The Octave of Angels

The Octave of Angels

Margaret McAllister

EERDMANS BOOKS FOR YOUNG READERS
GRAND RAPIDS, MICHIGAN / CAMBRIDGE, U.K.

Published 2002 by Eerdmans Books for Young Readers
an imprint of Wm. B. Eerdmans Publishing Co.
255 Jefferson Ave. S.E. Grand Rapids, Michigan 49503
P.O. Box 163, Cambridge CB3 9PU U.K.

Printed in the United States of America

02 03 04 05 06 07 7 6 5 4 3 2 1

Library of Congress Cataloging-in-Publication Data

McAllister, Margaret.
The octave of angels / written by Margaret McAllister.
p. cm.
Summary: After Calum and his family move to an English village at the time of an
ancient local festival, he finds that newcomers are not really welcome and he
uncovers several old village secrets.
ISBN 0-8028-5245-9
[1. Prejudices—Fiction. 2. Festivals—Fiction. 3. Secrets—Fiction.
4. England—Fiction.] I. Title.

PZ7.M11725 Oc 2002   [Fic]—dc21   200221610

For Mike and Pam Sellers
with love for and thanks for everything

One

Calum Lowry loaded his badminton racket and his camera into the trunk of the car because he wouldn't trust them to the moving men. It was a dull August day and he zipped up his jacket, huddling his chin down and his shoulders up until he squeezed into the back seat of the car with his sister and her bursting traveling bags. Then he wriggled to look out of the back window while Alexa twisted her face into scowls and told him to sit still.

He watched his old house until it was out of sight. Soon, he couldn't even see the town.

"Beckerton, next stop!" said his mother.

Calum had been to Beckerton before to stay with Aunt Dorcas. It was a great place for holidays. It would be all right, too, living there, if only he could take his friends, the sports complex, the cinema, the shopping center, the swimming pool, the bowling alley, and the burger place. But when your dad loses his job, your house is too expensive to keep, and you have an ancient great-great-aunt with a house too big for

1

her, there's only one obvious thing to do.

Beckerton. Sneeze, and you'll miss it. A few streets, a post office, a tiny shop with a tearoom, one church, a pub at each end of the village, and a duck pond. Oh, and a telephone booth. Plenty of guest houses, because every other cottage in Beckerton offered bed and breakfast.

Calum found he was watching for the sign, the one that stood at the entrance to the village so you could tell when you'd gotten there. There it was: *Beckerton – Historic Village. Please drive carefully.* The sign looked pretty historic, too. It was rusting around the edges. They drove past cottages hiding behind gardens full of hollyhocks and sunflowers, past the triangular village green with the pond full of sleepy ducks, up Church Lane—it was a short, steep climb—and parked outside Aunt Dorcas's house.

Calum had forgotten that it was a bit lopsided, and built of biscuit-colored stone. Purple flowers straggled over the windows as if they wanted to see what was going on inside. Hoisting his backpack over his shoulder he wandered up the path, weaving about to avoid bits of garden that were straying out of the flowerbeds, and long branches that caught on his jacket.

Aunt Dorcas! She was at the bay window looking older and tinier than ever, her face crumpled with the deep lines of age, her eyes twinkling with delight. Aunt Dorcas always looked as if she knew more than she would ever say. When she came to the door and held out her knotted hands, he saw that her back had become so stooped that he towered over her.

"So you're home at last!" she cried, and took his hands in her hard, knobbly fingers. "This is where you belong!" Then she added, as usual, "You must be hungry. Are you ready to eat?"

"We'd better unload first," he said, and went back to the car as Alexa and his parents picked their way through the weeds in the path. He was reaching into the trunk for his racket when, behind him, a voice cried out.

"Stop! Don't move!"

He looked around.

"I told you *not* to move!" insisted the voice, which was young, bossy, and female. "Mind your big feet!"

Calum looked down at his feet. A wrinkly brown toad was squatting just behind his right heel, nearly touching him. He stepped to one side to let it hop under the car, but it sat still, its throat pulsing, while it appeared to plan its next move. It made a half turn, stopped, stayed quite still as if it were counting, sprang towards the middle of the road, and stayed there.

It might have spent all day crossing the road, but Calum heard the approach of a truck. Darting into the road he scooped up the toad in both hands, grinning at its rough skin and silly, good-natured face — but before he could carry it to safety it had leaped at full stretch into the nearest hedge. There was laughter behind him as the moving van growled into sight and he turned to see a girl hurrying out of its way. She was smiling at the toad, not at Calum.

She was shorter and younger than Calum, with dark

3

corkscrew hair, very pink cheeks, and rough skin as if she'd dried herself quickly on a coarse towel. With a baggy sweater, trousers too big for her, and tall boots, she looked as if she'd come out for an evening bonfire party, not a summer morning.

"Was that your pet toad?" asked Calum.

"Pet toad?" She still sounded bossy. "Why would I want a pet one? I have got some tame ones in the garden, but they're not pets. Not really, not like cats and dogs and things. I just didn't want you to stand on him."

The van had parked, and the men were lowering the ramp. "Is that van yours?" she demanded. "Are you moving in? Where? Which house?"

"We're moving in with Mrs. Beeston," said Calum when he could get a word in, and added quickly, "She's my mom's great-aunt." He wanted to make it clear that they weren't complete newcomers.

"You lucky thing!" she said. "She's brilliant. She knows loads about birds and things. She gives . . . "

Calum found this was turning into one of those conversations where you have to fight to speak. "We're moving in so Mom can look after her and help her," he said, "and my dad's going to . . . "

"Calum! Come here and help!" yelled Alexa.

"See you!" called the girl. She stopped to stroke a cat as it arched ecstatically against her, then, as Aunt Dorcas appeared in the doorway, she waved a grubby hand. "Hi, Mrs. Peachstone!"

It sounded cheeky to Calum, but Aunt Dorcas waved back,

said, "Hello, Berry!" and moved aside to let the moving men through. "Calum, you'll want to see your room."

Aunt Dorcas understood things like that. She would know how he felt about his own room, and how he wanted to be all alone there for a few moments, before the furniture was in, while it was still as empty as a beach in winter.

"You've got the youngest legs," she said, "so I've put you in the attic."

Yes! thought Calum, who had always dreamed of an attic bedroom. He walked in slowly, treasuring the moment as he took possession of his kingdom, his footsteps echoing in its emptiness. Plain, white-painted walls sloped above his head, and the beams were dark as peat. From the window, he looked down into the village like a lord from a tower. To one side was the church, settled comfortably into its churchyard, and straight ahead, he could see across the moors. Far to the left was the forest, and hidden in its depths was Monksmoor House, which had once belonged to the wealthiest family in the area. That had been long ago. Now it was the very expensive Monksmoor Country House Hotel. Nobody without a Rolls-Royce ever got near it.

He couldn't see down into the valley, but he knew that the ruins of the old abbey still stood there with its ragged arches and massive sandstone pillars stretching up as if they wanted to touch the sun. There was a no-longer-used quarry on the moors, too, but Calum had always avoided it.

He remembered seeing that quarry long ago. It made a long gash across the moors, steep at one side and shallow at the other like a crooked smile. There was something threatening about it, like a monstrous jaw ready to swallow its prey. Long ago, a girl had been found dead at the bottom of that quarry. It should have been a good, scary story, but it had given him the creeps because it didn't have a proper ending. Nobody seemed to know how she came to be there. He couldn't remember that story very well, and he wasn't sure he wanted to.

"That's the bed for the attic," someone shouted, and the moving men clumped and clattered up the stairs.

✠   ✠   ✠

It was going to be a tight squeeze, getting everything into Aunt Dorcas's house. Nothing could be stored in the garage, because that was where Calum's father was setting up his electrical repair workshop. By the time evening became night, they were still surrounded by overflowing suitcases and bubble wrap. Aunt Dorcas carried a tray into the sitting room, weaving her way in and out of the obstacles, and put the dishes on the hearth because there was no room anywhere else.

"Who was that girl in the street?" Calum asked. "You called her 'Berry' and she called you 'Mrs. Peachstone.'"

"Berry, yes," she said, smiling. "Berry, short for Bernice. Bernice Carter. Her father works at White Fox Farm, and her mom helps in the farm shop. You two could be friends."

Calum wasn't sure. Berry was younger than he was and looked a bit odd, really. Besides, it seemed as if nothing with only two legs could be her friend.

"I see you brought your badminton racket," she went on. "Now, let me think. White Fox Farm, where Berry's father works, belongs to Drew and Peggy Fisher. They have a son, Mark, and I think he plays badminton. Yes, I'm sure he does. And young Octavia Shipley, I wonder if she plays?"

This sounded hopeful. "Will I meet Mark Fisher?" he asked.

"I expect so. Berry could introduce you."

"Berry called you 'Peachstone.' Why?"

She bent stiffly and picked up a downy peach from the bowl on the hearth. "Eat that, and you'll see," she said.

He smelled its sweetness before he bit into it. It tasted like its color, and he had to rub his hand across his dripping chin. He couldn't see what it had to do with Aunt Dorcas until nothing was left but the pit in his juice-stained hand. Stripped clean of every bit of fruit, it was deeply marked and lined and he could almost see a face in it, like the wrinkled face of a very old woman. Aunt Dorcas was looking at him with a face more crinkled than ever as she smiled.

"Peachstone," he said.

He had a start in the village now. There had always been Aunt Dorcas, and now he'd met Berry, too. Soon, he'd meet Mark Fisher, and he hoped they'd get along. Aunt Dorcas had mentioned somebody called Octavia, too—but she hadn't said much about her.

Two

In the morning he had to climb over tea chests to reach the bathroom, and getting to the kitchen was even harder. He would have liked to try Aunt Dorcas's stairlift, just for fun— she called it her heavenly chariot—but there was too much clutter on the landing for it to get through without jamming. She wasn't expecting to use it much, as she'd decided to live mostly on the ground floor. She even had her own bathroom, tucked into a corner of her bedroom. It had an alarm and handrails and was as pink and frilly as a party dress.

The house became more and more crammed as they unwrapped mountains of crockery and cutlery, pots and pans, clocks, cushions, more books than Calum could remember seeing in his life before, and a whole crate full of Christmas decorations. In the afternoon Mom announced that they all deserved a break, and she was taking Alexa into the nearest small town to go shopping. Calum quickly said he'd rather wander around Beckerton on his own, thank you.

Alone in the empty street, wondering what his friends

might be doing, he looked without interest into the windows of the village shop. There were postcards of the duck pond, with two ducks that might have been stuffed, and the slogan, *Beckerton – Home of the Octave of Angels.*

Beckerton – Home of Dead Ducks and Boring Postcards, thought Calum. If pocket money got a bit tight, which it probably would, perhaps he could design postcards for the village shop. *Beckerton – Home of Suicidal Toads, and Not Much Else.* The ducks on the pond had curled up to sleep.

He was wishing he'd gone shopping with Mom and Alexa when he noticed a small figure in the churchyard, bending over something. At first he could see nothing but faded jeans stretched over a very round bottom, but when the figure straightened and turned around he recognized Berry, her tangly hair trailing over her face as she examined something she was holding. Drawing nearer, he saw that she was standing near a very small grey tombstone, and that the thing moving feebly in her grubby hands was a hedgehog. A grey bobble, about the size of a bean, clung to its face, and there were more on its prickles.

"Shouldn't you leave it alone?" said Calum, knowing that wild animals shouldn't be handled.

"It's not well," she said firmly. "I found it by that special grave, you know, that little girl's grave, and she can't look after him, so I will. It's out in daylight, and it's covered in ticks. And it's all dopey and sorry for itself. It's doing poorly, aren't you, little one?"

Calum remembered something else about hedgehogs.

"Hasn't it got fleas?"

She gave him a look of contempt and pity. She didn't say *wimp*, but he could see her thinking it.

"We'll take it to the vet," she said. "She's at the farm this afternoon. I know, because Dad said so. He said she was coming to do some tests or something."

Calum fell into step beside her. "What's it like living on a farm?"

"This one's all right. Better than the last one. It isn't ours—Dad just works there. We haven't been here long. The people are really nice. There's Drew and Peggy—that's Mr. and Mrs. Fisher, who have the farm—and Mark. This way."

She did a sort of hopscotch step as she walked, repeating to the hedgehog, "Drew, Peggy, and Mark—Drew, Peggy, and Mark," as if she were trying to teach it a nursery rhyme. She stopped when Calum pointed out that she might be unsettling the hedgehog. They took the road towards the moors, Berry chattering all the time. Sometimes she talked loudly to Calum, and sometimes gently to the hedgehog.

"It's good at White Fox Farm," she said. "They don't use pesticides and all that, and they're kind to the animals. (There, there, hedgehog, don't wriggle or I'll get scratched) And Mom gets some lovely stuff to bring home from the shop. (Ouch) If we're lucky, they might be baking this morning. I like living here. They're going to do this thing in November that they do every year. It's called 'the something or other angels.' Ocky something."

"You mean, 'The Octave of Angels,'" said Calum.

"It has to do with a cart and dressing up," said Berry. "And there's a story about this boy."

"Berry," said Calum as patiently as he could, "my mother's family have always lived here. I can tell you all about the Octave of Angels, if you can keep quiet for a minute."

He wasn't sure if Berry had heard him, but he went on anyway. One of the good things about Beckerton was the Octave of Angels. He was already looking forward to it.

"It's about something that happened hundreds of years ago," he said. "There was a little kid who turned up in Beckerton at the end of November, and it was a really bad winter. Nobody knew who he was—he must have been a runaway—and he was all feverish and shivering so nobody would take him in. They thought he had the plague or something."

"That's cruel," she said.

"There was one big lad in the village who was kind to him. He was a bit simple, really, a bit of a village idiot, and he had a wheelbarrow that he used to take everywhere with him so he could do errands. He found the little kid, put him in the barrow, and wheeled him around the village trying to get someone to look after him. Nobody would, so he wheeled him to the abbey. It meant crossing the moors by night in winter."

"There'd be foxes and things," said Berry.

"And they believed in some spooky things in those days," he said. "Moorhags shrieking about and demon dogs. He got to the abbey, but by then the kid was so ill he died there. The

11

abbot was furious. He came to Beckerton with steam coming out of his ears and ordered the people to have eight days—that's an Octave—of fasting and prayer every November. Then they had to give money for the poor and walk to the abbey with it."

"What has it to do with angels?" asked Berry, speaking more to the hedgehog than to Calum.

"It doesn't. It used to be 'Angelus.'" The boy with the cart stayed at the monastery and they called him 'Brother Angelus.'"

"Do they still do all that walking and stuff?"

"Not now. Now it's more like a festival, and on the last evening they have a float. One of the village boys is dressed as Angelus, and he goes on the float to the abbey. Everyone else follows in cars."

"Who's going to be Angelus this year?"

"Don't know," said Calum, trying to sound casual. He knew it wouldn't be him, but he could dream.

Years ago as a small boy he had been to the Octave of Angels, standing in the drizzly darkness, watching the float jerk and jiggle away. The boy dressed as Angelus had stood there with the empty cart beside him. In the rough tunic, he had looked noble and alone. The abbey, when they reached it, had been a mysterious floodlit pool in the darkness and the boy had delivered his speech in a voice that rang and hung in the echoing arches. This Angelus had not been a shambling simpleton. He had become a hero, taken his place in Calum's heart, and stayed there with the unspoken wish—*I want to be him. One day.*

At a painted sign saying *White Fox Organics — Farm Shop* and an arrow, they turned along a well-churned-up farm track. Calum had to dodge about to miss the muddiest parts, but when he glanced up he saw a tall man waving to Berry. He had curly, receding hair, and wore overalls.

"Hello, Drew!" called Berry, and added needlessly, "That's Drew. It's his farm."

"Are you looking for your mom, Berry?" said Drew, as he strode towards them. "She's with Peggy in the kitchen."

"No, I'm looking for the vet. Is she here?"

"She's in the cowshed. What have you got this time?" Drew crouched down like a giant, telescoping himself to Berry's size. The hedgehog's eyes stayed closed, as if it felt too ill to face anything. "I'll ask her to look at it when she's finished with the cows. Who's your friend?"

Calum, anxious to get a word in before Berry could take over, explained who he was. Drew smiled broadly.

"I know your Aunt Dorcas. Berry, get a box from the store for your hedgehog and put it in the office. And wash your hands — you're a mucky little pup. Calum, do you want to come and wait in the shop?"

It wasn't much like a shop, more like a large shed bright with displays of fruit and vegetables. There were shelves of groceries, rows of fridges and freezers, and a door marked *Office*. Opposite Calum, at the far end of the room, behind a plate-glass window, was the kitchen, and from that kitchen came a glow of light and such a warm, earthy smell of baking that Calum's stomach felt hollow with hunger.

Two women in white aprons and hats were working there, patting fat white rolls of dough into shape and popping them onto trays. They were laughing and chatting to each other as they worked, and one of them glanced up, smiled, and waved to him with a floury hand as the office door opened and a boy appeared. The boy was a few years older than Calum, tall and curly-haired like Drew, and Calum knew he'd seen him before.

"Hi," said the boy, "you must be Calum. Dad said you were here. I'm Mark." He studied Calum's face for a few seconds, then smiled with recognition. "We're at the same school, aren't we? Baytree, in Westcastle."

The whole day brightened for Calum. Here was someone from his own world, and he had the feeling that he and Mark would get on. Things were getting better. The woman who had waved appeared at the kitchen door.

"Mark, come here!" she called, and she had a bright, kindly voice—a voice like a warm teacake, thought Calum, who couldn't help thinking of fresh bread. When Mark returned from the kitchen, he was carrying three honey-browned teacakes still steaming on a plate. They were fragrant, plump, and speckled with currants. Mark took one and held out the plate to Calum.

"Careful," he said, "they're still hot."

"Thanks!" Hardly believing his luck, Calum bit into the ·soft white bun that tasted as good as it smelled and even better than it looked. The kind-faced woman in the kitchen smiled at him. She looked as if she wanted to make the whole world happy with an everlasting supply of warm teacakes.

"That's my mom, making the teacakes," said Mark, "and that's Berry's mom helping her, the one who looks like a grown-up version of Berry. What year are you in at school?"

"Year Eight."

"Wish I was. I've got the exams coming up. Will you be going in on the school bus?"

"Suppose so."

"You'll get used to it. Eight o'clock from the duck pond on a winter morning. That means there'll be two of us to look out for Berry."

Two of us? Mark was talking as if they'd known each other for years, even as if they were the same age.

"Berry's starting at Baytree in September," Mark went on. "She used to go to the Catholic school, but it's too far to travel from here. It's a good thing you're around."

Calum started to ask why Berry needed anyone to "look out for her," but he had to stop when she appeared at the storeroom door, carrying a cardboard box with bits of straw sticking out of it.

"Go around the outside, Berry," said Mark. "No hedgehogs in the shop. There's a teacake here for you when you're ready." When she'd gone, he said, "We'll have to make sure she's all right at school."

"Why, what's the matter with her?"

"Nothing, but it's a new school for her, and she doesn't know anyone. Besides, you've seen what she's like. She'd

15

stand out in a crowd and get picked on."

"But Beckerton kids all stick together," said Calum. Everyone at school knew that. Beckerton kids were famous for it.

"Yeah, I've heard that one before," said Mark. "But that's the trouble. They do, and Berry isn't really a Beckerton kid. She's just moved in, she doesn't belong yet. The local kids won't stick up for her. They won't stick up for you, either, but you've already settled in at Baytree, so you don't need them."

There wasn't much bullying at Baytree school, but what there was consisted mostly of girls teasing anyone who lacked street-credibility. Calum could see why they'd pick on Berry.

"Why are Beckerton kids like that?" he asked.

Mark shrugged. "It's not just the kids. The adults think the world ends at the duck pond—or they wish it did." Berry, now without the hedgehog and with pinkly washed hands, came in and devoured her teacake.

"He's going to the animal sanctuary," she said, as soon as she could speak. "We're calling him Frank."

"Frank, the hedgehog?" said Calum.

"Short for frankincense," she said, and Calum doubled up with laughter.

"Why frankincense?" asked Mark.

"Because of where I found him," she said, pleased with herself. "I found him in the churchyard by that little girl's grave, and her name was Myrrh, like in gold, frankincense, and myrrh. So I called him Frankincense. He should have his name on his box. Have you got a pen?"

Mark handed her a felt pen from beside the till. "Be sure and bring it back," he called as she ran away. Calum was still laughing, but Mark wasn't.

"She doesn't understand about little Myrrh and what happened," he said. "If she did, she wouldn't be so daft about it. You'll know all about it, from Mrs. Beeston."

Calum didn't want to admit that he didn't know what Mark was talking about. But he'd find out. As he walked home, he was thinking again of postcards.

Beckerton, he thought, *Home of Toads and Teacakes.*

Beckerton: Home of Frankincense and Myrrh.

Home of Mad Toads and Dopey Hedgehogs.

Home of the Octave of Angels and

the Mystery of Myrrh.

Three

At home, he found Alexa struggling out of the car with bags of shopping and muttering some remark about "leaving me and Mom to do all the work as usual." Calum couldn't see why they'd gone shopping when there was enough to put away already.

After tea he arranged his books in tower blocks in his attic because he hadn't found his shelves yet. Aunt Dorcas had gone to a meeting at the other end of the village and eventually, bored with clearing up tissue and popping the bubble wrap, Calum went out to meet her. He saw her tired, rather sad face brighten into a smile as he waved to her.

"I went to White Fox Farm today," he said, falling into step beside her. "I met Mark Fisher, and Berry rescued a hedgehog." He told her about the afternoon, and went on, "So who was Myrrh? That can't have been her real name. Nobody's called Myrrh. Mark seemed to think I'd know about her."

"Myrrh?" She said the name slowly, as if it carried its own

18

sorrow. "Don't you know her story? Well, I suppose I should tell you. It's a pity the church is locked, or I could have shown you where the incense box would have been. But it's a fine evening, so we'll walk up there anyway."

In the churchyard, the shadowing of dusk was calling the bats from their tower. They swooped and flitted from the willows to the yew tree. She led him, slowly, steadily, to the plain little gravestone where, that morning, he had found Berry with the hedgehog.

"This is Myrrh's grave," she said, "poor little thing. My mother used to talk about her. They used to play together, when they were children."

They found a bench and sat there as the evening cooled. Calum watched the bats as Aunt Dorcas told him about Myrrh.

"First I need to tell you about the box, or it won't make any sense at all. The Octave of Angels was neglected for years. It just didn't happen. It was started again in 1872. The local squire in those days was Mr. Hetherington-Brooke—his family lived at Monksmoor House, which is the hotel now. He offered to pay for a village feast every year for the Octave, and suddenly the whole village decided it would be a good idea. He also gave the church a present. Do you know what this church is called?"

"I did once," said Calum, to give himself thinking time.

"It's the Church of the Epiphany," she said. "Three kings, gold, frankincense, and myrrh—that's the Epiphany. The new vicar was rather keen on incense, so Mr. Hetherington-Brooke gave him a beautiful wooden box decorated with gold to keep it in. Because it was valuable, it was only brought out on special occasions—over Christmas time, Easter, and the Octave of Angels. They gave it its own shelf beside the pulpit.

"Now, about Myrrh. Gypsies and tinkers often used to camp near Beckerton in those days. The Beckerton people didn't like them much, but to be quite honest, Calum, they've always been suspicious of everyone. The gypsies camped on the edge of the village on their way to the summer fairs, and sometimes stayed for the winter. They were here in 1892 at the beginning of the year, just about Epiphany time, and when they left the vicar found a baby, wrapped in shawls, lying on the church doorstep."

"A tinker's baby?"

"She was wrapped in one of their shawls, and there was a badly spelled little note pinned to it—"Her name is Murr." The vicar went after them, but they all refused to tell him anything about the baby, poor little thing. She was probably the child of a tinker girl and some man who couldn't or wouldn't marry her. The vicar and his wife adopted her. They supposed the mother had called her Myrrh because she was born at Epiphany. The village busybodies said it was a silly name and they should change it to Mary or Martha, but the vicar's wife said that Myrrh must keep her name because it was almost the only thing her own mother had given her. They put the spelling right though. Myrrh grew up rather shy, and not very bright. My mother liked her, but mostly the village children left her out of things, as the village children do."

Calum wondered if moving to Beckerton had been such a good idea. Aunt Dorcas seemed to understand.

"For you, Calum, it may be different. Your family is from Beckerton, and you're my nephew."

"I'm your great-great . . . "

"Oh, who cares how many greats it is? So, there was Myrrh, growing up in the village, a bit of a loner. If ever a garden was trodden on or a window broken or a gate left open, it was never one of the village children. Oh, no, it was Myrrh. Fortunately the vicarage family stood up for her. So did my mother.

"At the end of 1900, winter was so hard that snow and ice locked the village into itself. Everyone built up their log fires, ate Christmas cake, and told stories about the hags that haunt the moors and their fierce ghostly hell-hounds. On New Year's Eve in the morning, the doctor had to go out to Monksmoor House, because young Mrs. Hetherington-Brooke was having a baby. He got there, but if they'd sent for him any later he probably wouldn't have made it. The weather grew even harsher that night—mother said she could remember the wind screaming across the moors and whipping up the snow. That night, Myrrh went missing.

"They thought she might have done something naughty and gone to hide in a barn somewhere, but nobody could find her. In the morning, the vicar went to the church and found that not only Myrrh was missing. The precious incense box had gone, too."

21

"But that wasn't to do with her, was it?"

"Wasn't it?"

"But what would she want a box of incense for?"

Aunt Dorcas looked steadily at the little grey gravestone.

"Nobody will ever know that," she said. "Three days later, they found her dead at the bottom of the quarry with her neck broken."

Calum imagined ice, cold, and darkness. A child, lost and frightened, struggling through drifts so deep that frozen snow slipped inside her boots and soaked her feet. Did she cry? Did she shout for help? Did she try to turn back? And why was she out there at all? What was she trying to do?

"Did they ever find the box?" he asked.

"Yes, they found it," she said with a sigh. "It was beside her body, with the grains of incense spilling out."

"But why . . . ?"

"We don't know, and we never shall. The vicar and his wife said Myrrh must have had a reason for doing what she did, but they'd never know what it was. She was buried here, and they put up her little tombstone. And that, my boy, is that. I'm getting cold." She stood up so stiffly and slowly that Calum expected her to creak. "Give me your arm, Calum, for the walk home."

✟   ✟   ✟

By the time the new term started, Calum's family was settled in at Aunt Dorcas's house. His father had work coming in, but not enough of it, and his mother looked in the local

22

papers for a part-time job. She didn't want to work too many hours, she said. She wanted to be around when Calum and Alexa needed her, Dad might want help with setting up the business, and there was Aunt Dorcas to look after. Aunt Dorcas chuckled and said that she'd behave herself and try not to drop dead or burn the house down if she was left on her own.

Calum saw what Mark had meant about the Beckerton kids. Hanging around at the bus stop on the first day of term, it all looked perfectly friendly and innocent. Apart from himself, four kids in various school uniforms waited on the seat on the edge of the village green, beside the duck pond. One taller one leaned carelessly back against the phone booth. One wandered along deliberately late as if she didn't care whether she caught the bus or not. One, in a sharp new uniform, played some kind of hopscotch. But Calum, being part of it, knew better.

The four on the bench were all Beckerton kids. Two of them, who looked like sisters, sat on the bench putting in the earrings they weren't supposed to wear. Alexa was the one dawdling along. She was in the sixth form, and didn't want to be seen with a lot of kids. Mark, leaning against the phone box, was watching Berry play hopscotch on her own.

The other two on the bench were a fair-haired, very neat and pretty girl and a smaller boy, curly-haired, who must have been her brother. "Sit still, James," she kept telling him, or, "Are you cold?" or, "Remember, if you don't like your new teacher, tell me." She looked bored. When she wasn't nagging

23

James she was complaining about the bus being late.

"Who are they?" whispered Calum to Mark.

"Octavia and James Shipley, from Beckerton Hall," said Mark. "The Shipleys have lived here for generations."

"They don't go to our school, do they?" asked Calum.

"No way! They go to one of the private schools. They just travel on the same bus as the rest of us." Then James escaped from his sister and came to talk to Mark, while Octavia scowled. When James started talking to Calum, she called him away.

By the end of the first week, Alexa had agreed to sit in the aisle seat beside Berry, so that nobody could kick her schoolbag or push her on the way past as the bus filled up on the way to Westcastle. Sometimes Octavia joined in, hissing some cruel remark to Berry as she passed her, but more often she kept well away and conspicuously kept James away, too, as if Berry were contaminated and they might catch something. Mark and Calum sat behind Berry to protect her from hair-pulling and whispering. Calum was pretty certain that Berry neither knew nor cared how well they guarded her, but he liked the idea that he and Mark were brothers in arms. And by the end of September, there was the Octave of Angels to think about.

"Are you going to the Octave meeting tonight?" Calum asked Mark one afternoon, as they walked home from the bus.

"Why, are you?" Mark seemed surprised, and tried to hide it. He looked down as if he was talking to his shoes. "Don't expect too much. You should know what they're like by now."

At that point, Mark and Berry went on to the farm and Calum turned uphill into Church Lane. Octavia and James passed him, but this time, Octavia didn't try to avoid him. She moved very close to him, and whispered sharply in his ear.

"Poacher!" she whispered.

Was that really what she said? It couldn't be. What sense did that make? He looked around and saw her smiling as she walked away.

✠　✠　✠

The village hall was, to Calum, the most boring place he'd ever entered. It was whitewashed, with a stage at one end, no carpet, and drafts from the windows with their peeling paint. The chairs were so rocky you didn't dare sit back in them or you would topple over. There was a pinboard with notices like, "Join the Beckerton Ladies Musical Society — Why Not?," and "Please wash all cups and leave upside down on draining board," and "Please leave this hall as you found it," which didn't seem a very bright idea. Calum, Mark, and Berry sat at the back on a trestle table and played tic-tac-toe while they waited for things to start, and Calum tried to figure out who was who.

Octavia, with a tight blonde ponytail at the back of her neck, sat beside a sharp couple in very chunky sweaters and tight trousers. They reminded Calum of people in magazines who are pictured in fields with sheepdogs and labradors, but never get muddy.

"They're Octavia's parents," said Mark. "And the tall grey-

25

haired man with the moustache, the man at the front of the hall, that's Major Shipley. He's her grandfather. He's in charge of the meeting. And pretty well everything else around here."

Major Shipley stood as straight as if he had starched himself and propped himself up to dry. He had grey hair with a shiny patch at the front. He smiled warmly and laughed a lot, but Calum thought he wouldn't like to be argued with.

Near the front sat a row of women with short hair and little dark suits. They, said Mark, were mostly landladies—"And Mrs. Phipps from the shop," he added. "They really need the Octave for the tourist trade."

"The big one with the scary glasses is Mrs. Percy-Full, isn't she?" said Berry, too loudly.

"Shush!" said Mark sharply, and lowered his voice. "OK, if you two want a guided tour, listen. The one with the red hair and glasses like wing mirrors is Mrs. Percival. The very small, blonde woman next to her, in the tight suit, is Pat Parker. She has the guest house with hanging baskets outside, and the holiday cottages with the pink frilly curtains. Just think of Percival and Parker. Big Mrs. Percival, little Mrs. Parker."

"And there's the taxi woman," whispered Berry.

"That's Moira. Loud, bossy, drives the taxi. Calls her guests, 'my visitors.'" Mark lowered his voice and did a very passable imitation of a Beckerton landlady—"'My visitors always get their kettles and their teabags and their little pink soaps in their rooms. They always buy my raffle tickets, and I have them all checked out by ten o'clock.'" Calum supposed they wouldn't dare argue.

Then there was someone called Mrs. Phipps, from the shop, who had a worried look about her, and her husband, who looked blown about, as if he'd come in from the wind.

Berry looked along the row. "Percival, Parker, Moira, Phippses the shop," she chanted in a whisper. "Percival, Parker, Moira, Phippses the shop."

Drew and Peggy looked like real country people—Drew wearing a baggy old sweater and trousers splashed with mud, as if he'd only had time for a quick wash and a mug of tea after a day's work. Peggy turned to give them a big smile and a small wave. She looked entirely different without the baking hat and the white apron.

The meeting was called to order. Mark shushed Berry just a little too late as the room fell silent. "Percival, Parker, Moira, Phippses the—oops, sorry!"

Decisions were made about who would contact the newspapers and television and whether to lay on a supper in the village hall on the first night, and how much to charge. As soon as any decision was made, one of the landladies would say, "But what about . . . ?" or "Couldn't we . . . ?", and, "Why don't we . . . ?" and they had to start all over again. Calum and Berry gave up tic-tac-toe and played hangman instead. The Octave, it seemed, would begin with a church service, continue with concerts, parties, talks, and exhibitions, and would finish the following Saturday night with the flashlight procession to the abbey. For something they did every single year, it seemed to take a lot of discussion.

"And it'll end up the same as last year," said Mark quietly, and didn't attempt to hide a yawn. "It always does. Except that Dad's having some American students staying with us. That should be fun."

"All we need now," said Major Shipley at last, "is somebody to be Angelus. We thought we might already have an Angelus — or even Angela!" There was a murmur of polite laughter. "In these liberated days I'm sure nobody could object to a girl playing Angelus, but . . . " he smiled at the row of Shipleys at the front. Octavia's father stood up, turned to face the meeting, and spoke as if he knew everybody enjoyed listening to him.

"Yes, in spite of being named after the Octave of Angels," he said, "Octavia is not willing to be Angelus. She informs me that the costume tickles, it's cold, and she doesn't want to dress up as a boy. James is too young. Mark Fisher has done it before . . . "

Drew raised his hand. "Mr. Chairman!" he called, but Major Shipley didn't appear to notice. The discussion ranged over whether all the adults were too old, and Berry made a paper airplane out of the tic-tac-toe paper. Finally, Drew stood up.

"Mr. Chairman," he said loudly, so that everyone had to listen, "Dorcas Beeston's family has just moved back to the village. We should ask Calum Lowry to be Angelus."

Calum heard his name and felt his heart rise with hope. His dream had been spoken. But the hall was suddenly quiet with an unpleasant stillness, like the silence that follows the breaking of a window. Major Shipley avoided everyone's eyes.

"We've always felt it isn't fair to ask a newcomer to lead the procession," he said at last. "It really should be done by a lad who has spent most of his life in the village and has seen it done many times. A boy who's grown up with the Octave. We can't ask Calum yet."

Calum could tell what that meant. It meant, "we don't want to ask Calum." He'd never expected to be asked, but it was hard to see the door slam so firmly shut on his dream. Shut, locked, and bolted. It hurt so much he had to tell himself he didn't mind.

"Would you do it again this year, Mark?" said Major Shipley. Mark looked down at Calum.

"Go on," whispered Calum. "Go on. Please!" If it couldn't be him, he'd like it to be Mark.

Mark shrugged. "Yeah, no problem," he said.

The meeting was over. Calum and Mark jumped down from the trestle while Berry stayed there rescuing a spider she had found crawling in her hair.

"I suppose it's best if I do it," said Mark. "One year the church hall caretaker did it. The man over there." He nodded at an old man with a miserable expression. "The one with a face like a drain. You'll do it one day, Calum. You should, being a local family. That's why Dad tried to set it up for you."

"Yes, and it went down like a concrete parachute, didn't it?"

"They're scared of newcomers," said Mark. "Most of the families here tonight are Beckerton families, not newcomers.

29

There are plenty of them about, but the village people resent them."

"Why?"

"Why do you think?" asked Mark, as if Calum had just asked why birds didn't like cats. Then he smiled again. "You don't know much about the country. Every time a cottage comes up for sale it's bought by rich townies, usually ready to retire. Loads of people here tonight have grown-up children who had to move out of the village and bring up their kids in town, because they can't afford the houses here. That's why there are so few kids around. And Beckerton people can't seem to trust newcomers."

"Aunt Dorcas said they never could," said Calum.

Mark laughed. "And my mom would say they won't welcome strangers, 'till the snow catches fire,' as they say around here."

"Octavia certainly won't," said Calum. "She called me a poacher today, I don't know why."

"Memories last too long around here," said Peggy Fisher's voice behind him. She put an arm around him, and gave a quick squeeze to his shoulders. "Don't worry about it, Calum. It's all in the past."

"What's all in the past?" he asked, but she didn't hear him as, at that moment, he had to step backwards. He and Mark squeezed up against the trestle to give the Shipleys room to get out.

"Did they really call you Octavia after the festival?" asked Calum, as Octavia walked past.

30

"Oh, yes," she said coolly, and stopped to look him in the eyes. "My aunt is Octavia, too. It runs in the family. Why didn't they call you *Bagshaw?*" Then she smiled as if she had said something very witty and stalked out of the hall.

Calum looked at the Fishers. "Bagshaw? What was that about?" he asked. Peggy looked at Drew, Drew looked at Calum, and Mark looked at the floor.

"Don't you know, dear?" asked Peggy. "Perhaps you should ask . . . "

"I know," he sighed. "Ask Aunt Dorcas."

"And ask your dad to give me a ring," said Drew. "I've got a generator that needs looking at."

Beckerton, thought Calum on the way home.

Home of Myrrh and Mystery.

At least there was a chance of some badminton, if Mark or somebody would play.

Beckerton for . . . what had Octavia said?

Bagshaw?

Four

Aunt Dorcas went to bed early, so there was no chance to ask her what Octavia had meant. Even Peggy had hinted at a dark secret in his family's past, but nobody would tell him what it was. He tried not to think about it that night but it kept him awake so that he slept late into the morning and came down when everybody else had finished breakfast and gone out. Only Aunt Dorcas was in the kitchen, rinsing the blue and white teapot.

"Hi, Great-aunt Peachstone," he said.

"Oh, so you're up now? Get yourself some breakfast, then. Alexa's out somewhere, and your parents are at White Fox Farm." She put on the kettle and chose a delicately flowered china cup for herself and a chunky mug for Calum.

Calum made toast and buttered it, and when the tea was made, he said, "There's something I need to know about our family."

She tucked in her chin like an indignant little bird and brought the cups to the table. Her papery old hands trembled as she poured the tea—but then, they always did.

"Now, what can you want to know?" she asked.

"It's something Octavia Shipley said." He watched her face. "She called me 'poacher.'"

"Oh, I am clumsy!" exclaimed Aunt Dorcas as tea splashed into her saucer. She mopped it up with a cloth and seemed determined not to answer him until she'd finished.

"And yesterday, after the meeting," went on Calum, "she said that the name 'Bagshaw' should run in our family. The Fishers were a bit embarrassed."

"Yes, well, they probably thought you knew," she said. "She means Samuel Bagshaw." She folded her hands around the flowery teacup. "Samuel Bagshaw was my grandfather, and your goodness-knows-how-many-greats grandfather. I don't remember him—he died long before I was born. Yes, he was a poacher. Lots of country people were, you know. He made himself a little too much at home on the Monksmoor Estate, when the Hetherington-Brooke family lived there. He had one of those special jackets with hidden pockets for hares and rabbits and birds, of course."

"But what did he *do* ?"

"As I said, a bit of poaching—or a lot of poaching. What he couldn't use himself, he sold. It's said that he dealt in other stolen goods, too, but nothing was ever proved. When you've washed the butter off your hands, look in the sideboard. Left hand side. There's a toffee tin with photographs in it."

He found the tin and, after a lot of shuffling through pictures of stiffly smiling wedding groups and Calum's mother when she was a baby, Aunt Dorcas lifted out a tatty, yellowing photograph. It showed a lean, dark-haired young man with a moustache. Beside him, a large-eyed young woman with curly hair held a baby in her arms, and a dog lay at his feet. It was a dark, shaggy dog, its head raised, its wary eyes on the camera.

"That's him," she said, "Samuel Bagshaw. And the baby is my father, Frank."

"Nice dog," said Calum.

"Ah, but take a good look at him. He's a lean, long-bodied black dog. Perfect for slipping through the undergrowth at night without being seen. A real poacher's dog."

"But," said Calum, "I got the feeling that there was something *really* bad about him. It was as if Octavia wanted me to be ashamed."

"Nonsense," she said. She pushed the photographs into their tin and pressed down the lid. "Though he was a bit of a — what would you say? — bad lad. Fond of his drink, and too ready with his fists. My poor grandmother — you can't see any bruises in that photograph, but she didn't have a happy life with him. Not an ancestor to be proud of. My father never talked about him."

"What happened to him?"

"He left Beckerton in 1900 — left his wife and son, too — and died a few years later. His wife stayed here. Frank got a scholarship to the grammar school. Later, he owned the first motor car in the village — apart from the Hetherington-Brookes, of course — and was the only taxi for miles around."

34

"Yes, but . . ."

"Finish your tea and put the photographs back," she said, so he did. He knew she hadn't told him the whole truth and she wasn't going to, not yet. Presently he heard the car returning, and knew from his parents' voices that something good had happened.

"That was a good morning's work!" said his mother. "What nice people!" His father put a large cardboard box on the kitchen table. It had a picture of green apples, and "all organic produce" was printed on the side.

"It's a welcome present from the Fishers," said his mother, unpacking a homemade quiche, still warm from the oven, and a carrot cake. Then there were apples and pears, potatoes and carrots, smooth, firm tomatoes and wide round mushrooms ridged with dark gills.

"And that's not all," she said, "Paul fixed the generator, and they want him to go back and have a look at a washing machine, too."

"Paid up front," said Dad.

"And," said Mom, "they need more staff in the shop at busy times, and Peggy can't do the baking and serve customers at the same time. I'll be working three or four half days in there, starting next week."

✦　✦　✦

"The cake was great," said Calum to Mark on the bus home on Monday. "When my mom starts work at your shop, I could walk along from school with you and Berry sometimes, to

35

meet her."

"And sit in the shop eating teacakes?" said Mark, and grinned. "Mom won't mind. And Dad's very keen for you to get involved in the Octave, if you want to."

"I do want to," he said, but he lowered his voice in case Octavia was listening. "I could carry a flashlight in the procession or something. What about Berry?" Berry was gazing dreamily out of the window.

"Berry?" said Mark. "Do you want to be in the Octave procession?"

Berry turned towards him wide-eyed, as if she was bringing her daydreams with her.

"Only if I can bring my dog," she said.

"You haven't got a dog," said Calum.

"I will, after the weekend," she said smugly. "We're going to the Rescue Center. To rescue one. But it mustn't chase any other animals or I'd have to rescue those, too."

"How's Frank, the hedgehog?" asked Calum.

"He's getting better. He'll hibernate soon." When the bus stopped, she wandered off to stroke a cat on a wall.

"Calum," said Mark, "you know the other night—what Octavia said about the poacher . . . "

"It's no problem," said Calum. "Aunt Peach . . . Aunt Dorcas told me about Samuel Bagshaw."

"Nothing was proved," said Mark. "Nobody ever knew what happened, but villages need to have someone to talk about. They don't get many mysteries, so they still dig up the story about that night."

What night? wondered Calum, but it would be no use asking Mark. He'd only tell him to ask Aunt Dorcas. Berry came back with the cat following her, its tail in the air.

"Anyone want to come back for a game of badminton?" asked Mark.

"Badminton!" said Calum.

"We've got an old barn we can use. Dad's turning it into a camping barn, but at this minute, it's just a big empty space with a net in it."

"I'll get my racket," said Calum.

Not much had been done to the barn, but it had a wooden floor, windows, and electricity from a generator. The game of badminton wasn't all Calum had hoped for. Mark was a very good player when he was there to play at all, but he kept disappearing to help in the shop. Berry loved taking his place, but as she couldn't hit a shuttlecock if it came at her slowly, she wasn't much of an opponent. Still, it was a chance to play, and that was something. Not quite Westcastle Leisure Center, but something. And the friends he had here were good friends.

✠   ✠   ✠

On Saturday morning Aunt Dorcas was, as usual, down before him. She wore her old tweed coat, and was coming in from the garden with branches of berried hawthorn and a bunch of windblown yellow chrysanthemums to decorate the church for harvest festival. Calum carried the branches to the church for her — there were so many that he had to keep peering around to see where he was going.

"It's a waste to take apples and pears to harvest festival," she said as they walked to church. "They roll off windowsills and get covered in dust, then after Sunday they're picked up, all bruised and gritty, and sent out as presents to old people who don't want to eat them anyway because their teeth aren't up to it."

"You're not one of the old people, are you?" grinned Calum. The eyes in the peachstone-crinkled face were bright with humor.

"I've told them to send my share to the Homeless People's Center in Westcastle," she said. "Much more sensible." They were in the graveyard now, and he pushed the branches aside so he could see the little grave. The grass had been kept short around it, and the one word, *Myrrh,* showed clearly. In front of it was a gleam of bright yellow.

"Somebody's put flowers on Myrrh's grave," he said.

"Of course they have," she answered carelessly. "Put your back against the door and heave. It's so heavy."

He hadn't been inside Beckerton church for years, but he remembered it was old-fashioned and smelled of age and furniture polish. Visitors who came for the Octave went to the church to see the frescoes, the wall paintings, high on the stone arches. They were famous, those paintings. And there were carved wooden mice on the pews and pulpit.

There was a purposeful air in the church. All the Shipleys were there, dressing the font with fruit and flowers so busily that they made Calum think of traders setting out a market

38

stall. He sat and looked around at the deep baked-brown wood of pews and pulpit. The stone was patchy and changing, some pale honey colored, some like rough oatmeal. A polished wooden rail gleamed in front of the altar. There was a mouse carved into the rail—Calum couldn't see it but he knew where it was, on the other side, running down the upright. He stepped back to take a better look at the frescoes.

There were shepherds and angels on one side, the three kings on the other, and, high above the central arch that joined them, the Bethlehem stable. A sweet-faced Mary, a bearded Joseph, and small children and animals gathered around the manger. The shepherds wore brown-bread-colored tunics and angels swooped and worshipped, white in a midnight sky, but the kings were splendid with color. He could remember gazing and gazing at them when he had been a little boy. They wore robes of purple and scarlet, and carried jewelled treasure boxes in their hands. Even the camels' bridles were braided with gold, and the kings' three young servants were brightly dressed. But it was the faces that fascinated him most.

"Calum!" called a voice behind him. He jumped, and Octavia sniggered. Drew Fisher was carrying in something wrapped in tissue paper.

"Sorry, son! I didn't mean to give you a fright. Were you looking at the frescoes?"

"I like the kings. When I was little I always watched them in case they moved when I wasn't looking."

"Did you know they're all real people?" asked Drew. Calum did know, but he didn't mind Drew telling him about it again. "They were done about a hundred years ago, by a local artist, and the Beckerton folk were his models. You see the shepherd second from the end, with the funny face? That's Peggy's grandfather."

"Aunt Dorcas says the tangly-haired angel is her mother," said Calum. "Is Myrrh in there anywhere? She should be."

Octavia and her family, busy with their decorations, suddenly stopped talking. Octavia was staring at him — then she whisked around and whispered something to James.

"No, she's not," said Drew in a matter-of-fact way. "She would have been. She was going to be the third king's servant, naturally."

"What about any more of my family?" asked Calum, and saw Octavia's eyes and mouth widen in astonishment.

"Not as far as I know," said Drew, and changed the subject. "Do you want to know what I've brought with me? James, do you want to see?"

Drew unwrapped the tissue. There was a fresh smell of bread and from the crumpled paper appeared a golden brown sheaf of wheat, every ear shaped and baked into its place, each stalk neatly rolled and marked.

"A harvest sheaf!" said Calum.

"It's got a mouse," said James.

"Two mice," said Drew. One fat little bread mouse perched on an ear of wheat, and another ran up the stalks. "Peggy makes one every year. She'll call on your mom soon, Calum, to sort out her working hours. We want her settled in before the Octave starts. It gets busy then. She might help with our

40

students, too."

"Students?" said Octavia's mother, sharply.

"Yes, American students. There's a group of them studying at the university in Westcastle, they came earlier in the year to look around the farm. They want to see the Octave, so I said they could stay in our barn. I'm turning it into a camping barn, so this'll make me get a move on. You kids can still play badminton in there until they arrive."

It became quiet again, so that Calum wondered what had been said to upset somebody this time. Then he noticed the little group of women by the door, the landladies who hoped to make a profit from visitors to the Octave, regarding Drew with wary, suspicious faces.

"We don't mind you taking visitors, Drew," said Moira, loudly. "But you can't go undercutting our prices. We've agreed on the rate for bed and breakfast."

Drew laughed. "Don't worry, Moira. They're just students. They couldn't afford bed, let alone breakfast at your prices. They just want to slum it in the barn. And they're a good bunch. I took a liking to them."

"Oh, I do hope it won't be all chewing-gum and those awful hats," sighed Octavia's mother.

"So long as they don't go wandering out over the moors at night," said Octavia innocently. "You never know what might happen. Somebody could get killed."

"Octavia!" said her father sharply. "Ignore her, Calum."

What was he supposed to ignore? This village was full of secrets that he was only half-told. Aunt Dorcas came over,

41

brushing bits of twig from her coat.

"That'll do for now," she said. "Shall we go home, Calum?" Walking out of the churchyard, they nearly tripped over a short, shaggy, black-and-tan hearthrug of a dog surging towards them, dragging Berry at the end of its lead.

"Isn't he wonderful!" panted Berry through the straggles of hair falling across her face. "His name's Wow! He's so lovely!"

Beckerton, thought Calum. *Home of Ghost Dogs and Mutts. Mongrels and Moorhags.* Come to think of it, what was a moorhag supposed to look like?

Home of lots of things, but nobody will tell me what they are.

Five

By the time Wow had rushed at them, dashed about in circles, wrapped his lead around a tree, tripped over it, and been rescued by Berry, Calum felt they'd been well and truly introduced. Berry was gabbing unstoppably.

"He put his paws up on his cage," she said, "and I asked him his name and he said, 'Wowowow!' He likes me. He likes you, too."

"I hope he calms down," said Aunt Dorcas, but she was smiling.

"He's just excited today because everything's new," yelled Berry over her shoulder as Wow hauled her around. Aunt Dorcas chuckled quietly.

"I'll light the coal fire tonight," she said, "and I can tell you about poachers and dark secrets. Really, this village!"

"At last!" said Calum.

It became a full day. Dad was called out by a large family with a broken-down washing machine. Peggy phoned to ask Mom if she'd like to go and spend the afternoon at the shop, and could she start work this week, please? Calum went with her and helped Mark carry crates of fruit from the store. When it was time to go home, Peggy glanced at her watch and opened the till.

"Two hours, Calum," she said. She took his hand, dropped some money into his palm, and folded his fingers over it.

"What's that for?"

"You've been working, haven't you? Or did the moorhags lift all the crates? They're not usually so helpful."

"I didn't do it for money," he said.

"Call it a bit of pocket money, then. With the Octave and Christmas coming, we'll need extra help. And there's the bonfire party before all that, and the barn to get ready for the students. They're looking forward no end to the Octave; they don't have anything like it in Minnesota." She slipped some teacakes into a bag. "Take those home. And take those yogurts in the fridge, the ones with the yellow top. They're getting near their date, and I doubt I'll sell them now."

✛ ✛ ✛

In the evening, Calum carried coffee and toasted teacakes into Aunt Dorcas's room.

"What exactly is a moorhag like?" he asked.

"A moorhen? Swims and quacks."

"Moorhag," he said loudly, knowing she was teasing. "I know it's a kind of ghost."

"It's our favorite local ghostie. People around here used to believe in them, sort of screeching women on the moors.

Sometimes they have scary hairy dogs with big luminous eyes, even worse than that thing of Berry's. Moorhags are supposed to be a warning of death. They're more likely to be a warning of what will happen to a farmer staggering home on a stormy night too drunk to tell a ghost from a tree."

Calum laughed, but he couldn't help wondering if there was any truth in it. He licked butter from his fingers, and said, "Aunt Dorcas—Peachstone—I wish you'd tell me *everything* about Samuel Bagshaw. There must be more to his story than anyone's told me. He's like a shadow on the village. And on me."

"There are worse shadows than Samuel Bagshaw on this village," she said in a quiet, cross way, more to her teacup than to Calum. She put the cup on the hearth and wriggled back in her chair. "Well, I'll tell you," she said with a sigh, "but there's not much to tell. He was a poacher, he was violent, he liked a drink—you knew that. And you know that Myrrh disappeared on a wicked Old Year's Night and was found dead in the quarry with the incense box. She wasn't the only person on the moor that night, Calum. Sam Bagshaw was out, too."

"I thought it was such a bad night that nobody else went out."

"A few brave souls struggled over to their neighbors' houses to welcome the New Year. Most of them admitted they'd seen something on the moor, but nobody was sure what. Some insisted it was a moorhag. They all said they'd seen an animal, and some thought it was Sam's dog. Some thought they'd seen Sam, but in that light, it was hard to be certain. There were human and animal prints in the snow, but the vicar and his friends had gone out early with their dogs to look for Myrrh. There were criss-crosses of footprints and pawprints, and who could tell whose they were?

"After Myrrh was found, the police questioned Sam Bagshaw. He swore he hadn't been out, but Sam would swear to anything. They searched the cottage and there was no evidence of anything illegal—not even a hare hanging up, or a pheasant hidden up the chimney. But it looked very strange that, on the night Myrrh ran away with the incense box, he was on the moors, too."

Coldness prickled the back of Calum's neck. "Did they think he murdered her?"

"He might have done it, if he had a reason for it," said Aunt Dorcas. "The police seemed to think that—well, that Sam and Myrrh had plans to be out at the same time."

"So they thought that Myrrh and Sam Bagshaw had arranged the theft between them?" said Calum, trying to work it out. "It doesn't seem likely."

"Sam wasn't liked, and Myrrh was a tinker's child. The village believed the worst of both of them. One theory was that Sam ordered her to steal the box for him and then killed her so she'd never inform against him. A second idea was that he saw her steal it and went after her to get it for himself. Or, she might have stolen it and tried to sell it to him, knowing that he dealt in stolen property."

"What do *you* think?"

46

"I think my grandfather was altogether a nasty piece of work," she said. "If Myrrh had been the vicar's own daughter, everyone would have made excuses for her, but not for the little tinker. Beckerton is like that."

He wanted to say that it wasn't. He liked to see Beckerton as he saw it from the school bus in the afternoons—a place of shelter, with its warm cluster of stone buildings among the wild moors and forests. Now that the evenings were drawing in, the lights of houses up and down the village made it secret and welcoming at the same time. Maybe it was a mixture of good and bad, like most people.

"Perhaps Sam stole it," he said, "and was on his way to hide it until he could sell it. Myrrh saw him, followed him, and fought him to get it back."

"All the way to the quarry? No, I'm afraid it does look as if Myrrh took it." She rubbed crumbs from her creased fingertips. "It's not that unlikely, Calum. Myrrh was . . . " She took a deep breath and seemed to hold it as she hunted for the right word. "Different," she said at last, and sighed.

"But she didn't steal, did she?" said Calum.

"It depends on what you mean by stealing. She liked taking flowers to the vicar's wife, and to anybody else who was kind to her. She never seemed to understand the difference between wild flowers in a meadow and the roses growing in other people's gardens. She gave candles to anyone she thought might need them—the church's candles, usually. You can laugh, my boy, but it did cause a lot of annoyance and Myrrh couldn't seem to see what was wrong

47

with it. She took a petticoat from someone's washing line to give to mother, because it was pretty. Myrrh always kept some of her dinner to feed to the garden birds. Rice pudding and mashed potato! She seemed to think that giving away the church's candles was just the same."

"So she only stole things to give away?"

"Oh, yes, but if anything went missing, from a sausage to a sovereign, Myrrh was suspected."

"Then, if she took the box, she meant to give that away, too," said Calum triumphantly.

"It's the sort of thing she'd do, but she wasn't likely to meet anyone who wanted it. Not on the moor in the middle of a winter night. To this day, nobody knows what happened that night. These days, everyone feels sorry for Myrrh—but if another child like her turned up in the village, they'd be just the same."

"Whatever she did, she can't have meant any harm," said Calum. "I want to prove that she was innocent. She was a misfit, like Berry, and I want everyone to like her."

"Hmph!" snorted Aunt Dorcas. "They don't like anyone if they can help it. They don't even like each other much but they stand together against the world, and it'll be the same till the snow catches fire. Don't fool yourself, Calum. The Octave of Angels has nothing to do with being sorry for letting a child die. It has to do with throwing our doors wide open to visitors and coaxing as much money out of them as possible."

The lines in her face seemed to be carved from rock. Then she smiled, and her face softened and became a peachstone again.

"Here I am, talking like a bitter old woman, and I'm not, not really," she said. "But I can see what the Octave ought to be. Big hearts and warm welcomes. Instead, it's souvenir mugs and profit margins and charging extra for full breakfasts. Goodnight, Calum."

Calum lay awake that night thinking of Myrrh, the box, and Sam Bagshaw. If Myrrh was out that night, she must have had a good reason. Sam Bagshaw almost certainly had a bad one. Too bad that he was Calum's ancestor. The truth, whatever it was, had to be found.

Beckerton – Home of Bagshaws and Badminton.
      Home of the Octave of Angels –
        of Poachers –
        of Secrets –
      The Octave of Secrets.

$\mathcal{S}_{ix}$

Autumn grew colder, and Calum became more and more familiar with the village. Berry was happy at school, but school was a thing she hardly seemed to notice. Calum often saw her as he looked down from his high window first thing in the morning. On cold days her cheeks were redder than ever, and her nose, too, and she was always beaming as she galloped down the lanes with Wow pulling ahead. Often she came running for the school bus as it was arriving at the stop. Those were the mornings when she'd spent too long racing around the lanes with Wow. Octavia would stand well back, and keep James back, too, to avoid touching her.

When Mom was working at the farm shop, Calum went there with Mark and Berry after school. On busy days, he and Mark would throw their school bags into the office and help in the shop. At other times, as November approached, they helped to build the village bonfire in a field behind the farmhouse. Peggy always slipped Calum a cheese scone or a teacake, or tucked a bar of chocolate into his pocket. "And you've earned that," she would say, curling his fingers around the money she pressed into his hand.

He had imagined the whole village working together for the Octave, but as it came nearer he found that it didn't do anything of the kind. The landladies worried if anyone charged the visitors less than they did. Mrs. Phipps at the tea shop was upset because the church ladies were providing afternoon teas in the church hall. Aunt Dorcas was outraged at the cost of the official souvenir book.

The caretaker at the abbey ruins disapproved of the Octave altogether. He complained that it was all very good fun if you happened to live in Beckerton, but as far as he was concerned it meant opening the abbey late in the evening. And if you asked him, but nobody did, it was just an excuse for getting in free. One thing everyone agreed on was that Drew and Peggy were making a great mistake in filling their barn with American students.

Calum heard Mrs. Shipley talking about it to Pat Parker, one of the landladies, after church. At the time he was crawling under a pew trying to reach a dropped hymn book, but he recognized Mrs. Shipley by her voice and Pat by her shoes. Nobody else in Beckerton wore heels as high as that.

"It's not a question of the money," Mrs. Shipley was saying. "It's just not the Octave sort of thing." Calum thought that welcoming strangers was exactly the Octave sort of thing, but as he was wedged under a pew with his face a centimeter from the dusty floor, he couldn't say so.

"The thing is," came the tinny voice of Pat Parker, "we

have regular visitors who know what to expect from the Octave. They want the hymns, the procession, and all that. They pay for tradition. Not for a lot of gum-chewing backpackers taking over the place and saying 'gee' every other word. They won't understand it. I think—"

She stopped sharply. Calum, under the pew, saw a pair of large feet in old but well polished shoes stride past. Drew Fisher's feet. He wriggled to get out, but his own foot was wedged solidly between the bottom of the pew and the floor. He had no idea how he'd got it there, but it wasn't going to move. He tugged hard.

"Morning, Drew." It was Moira this time. Calum thought she must know a lot of deaf people and was used to shouting. "I was hoping to come and see you at the farm shop to arrange for the Bonfire Night Party on Friday. Mrs. Percival and I are organizing it this year, as Mrs. Shipley has so much to do."

"What is there to organize?" said Drew. "It's all prepared, as far as I know."

"I was thinking about sausages," said another voice— Calum knew it was Mrs. Percival. Calum could imagine her simpering, with her head tilted to one side. "I don't suppose we could negotiate a discount on some of your delicious farm sausages?"

"Peggy and I always provide the sausages for Bonfire Night," said Drew, "free and for nothing. It's our contribution."

With a teeth-gritting heave Calum yanked his foot free

from the pew. His shoe stayed behind. He heard it roll over as it fell and he struggled to his feet.

"What on earth have you been doing? Crawling around among the cobwebs?" boomed Moira.

"Yes," said Calum and handed the book to Drew, who was collecting them. Pat Parker brushed him down firmly, and he flinched. What made it worse was that Octavia and James, bored and waiting for their parents to stop talking to people, were watching.

"You'll all come on Bonfire Night, won't you, Calum?" said Drew. "Pat, stop fussing at him; he hates it. Hot dogs and fireworks in the field behind the small barn. Bring your boots; it'll be muddy."

"We can sell mulled wine at eighty pence a glass," said Mrs. Percival brightly.

"No, we couldn't, because there's enough expense at this time of year already," said Drew. "There'll be a box for donations to the cost of fireworks, and that's all."

Pat Parker strutted forward and looked as if she was about to say something—but with a lurch she tripped forward as if she were falling over a cliff, her arms outstretched and her mouth open like a goldfish. Drew, reaching forward to catch her, lost control of the pile of books he was carrying, which toppled to the floor with a drum roll of thuds.

"Who left that shoe lying there?" snapped Pat.

"Oops," said Calum. "Sorry." Drew picked up the shoe from the floor, and Calum bent his head over it to hide his hot face while he pretended to be tying the laces.

When he looked up, Octavia's eyes were on him, full of laughter. Of course she'd laugh. Then, to his surprise, he saw that it was friendly laughter, as if Pat falling over was a shared joke.

✠   ✠   ✠

Bonfire Night was dry and bitterly cold. The towering bonfire was watched by huddled crowds wrapped in layers of scarves and hats. Calum kept warm by hurrying from the shop to the bonfire with trays of hot dogs and soup. Against the darkness, the bonfire roared and crackled with flame like an angry dragon, casting wild fiery light on wide-eyed faces. Shredded gold poured from Roman candles. Rockets spilled a crash of colors into the sky, and the air was filled with the pungency of gunpowder smoke and fried onions. When the flames leapt, Calum could see Aunt Dorcas so wrapped up in her warmest clothes that she looked like a Russian doll.

He took a tray of hot dogs to the Shipley family. "You're still one of the poacher's lot," said Octavia softly, but she didn't sound as superior as usual. She certainly didn't look it, with a woolly hat on and tomato soup on her chin. Calum went back to the shop to refill the empty tray.

"Where's Berry?" he asked Mark. "She was here earlier, checking the bonfire for hedgehogs."

"She's staying in with the dog," said Mark. "She said he'd be scared. She'd given him a tranquilizer, but she still wanted to stay with him. I took her a hot dog."

"She's probably fed half of it to Wow," said Calum. "I'll

take her another one." At the farm cottage, Berry dragged him in, and shut the door quickly.

"I need to keep the door shut," she said, "so Wow can't hear the noise."

Wow didn't look able to hear anything. He lay sprawled across the carpet, half-opening his eyes when Calum came in.

"His tranquilizer's working," said Calum.

"He still needs me here," said Berry. "It might wear off. Dogs hate fireworks; they scare them."

They watched the fireworks from the window until Calum went back to the farm to help the Fishers clear up. When he finally got home, cold and smelling of woodsmoke, he found everyone drinking tea in Aunt Dorcas's sitting room.

"The best fireworks display ever," said Aunt Dorcas with satisfaction. She stroked her cup with papery fingers. "Mother said there were wonderful fireworks at Monksmoor House the night the young heir was born, but of course she saw them from a distance."

"Hang on, Aunt Peachstone. What are we talking about?" asked Calum.

"Calum!" said Mom. "What did you call Aunt Dorcas?"

"I like it," said Aunt Dorcas, smiling with her eyes shut. "It suits me. Berry thought of it first. Calum, you seem so much to belong here, I forget you don't know all the bits and pieces of the stories. Didn't I tell you about the new baby, the night Myrrh disappeared?"

Calum suddenly remembered. "You said the doctor had got through to Monksmoor House to deliver a baby."

"Oh, everyone was so excited about that! In a village like this, at the end of the nineteenth century, the people at the big house were like royalty. Young Mrs. Hetherington-Brooke was having her first baby. At about nine o'clock on New Year's Eve, the vicar reported that the baby had been born, and it was a boy."

"How did he know?"

"Oh, there was a signal arranged. A lantern from the roof of the house. One flash for a boy, two for a girl. The vicarage family and the servants were taking turns to look out for it. The vicar ordered rum punch all around and lemonade for the children, to drink to the baby's health. Later, there were fireworks from the big house, and they even fired guns into the air to celebrate. How the baby and his mother were supposed to get any sleep, I can't imagine."

"It was New Year's," said Dad. "I suppose the fireworks were meant for midnight, but they set them off early. Calum, you've had a long day. Don't you want to go to bed?"

"I'm not tired."

"No, but I am," said Aunt Dorcas. "And it's my bedtime, but your father is too polite to say so."

Calum went upstairs and turned off the light. He looked into the night from his angled attic room, like an astronomer from a tower. Orion sprawled across the night with Sirius bright at his heel, and all the stars he couldn't name were scattered across the sky as if they had been thrown there. In three weeks, they would shine on the Octave of Angels.

There was a tap at the door and Aunt Dorcas peeped

around it, out of breath from struggling up the attic stairs. In the light from the landing, she looked like an old woman in a fairy tale.

"Not in bed yet?" she whispered. "Drew Fisher just phoned. He asked if you'd like a trip to the abbey on Sunday afternoon. He wants to check a few things for the Octave. If you want to go with him, you're to go straight to the farm after Sunday lunch."

✙   ✙   ✙

Berry and Mark were to go to the abbey, too. Trying out Mark's voice in the abbey ruins was one of the main reasons for going. Berry had agreed to leave Wow at home. He wouldn't have been allowed in the abbey ruins, and the car might have seemed crowded with him in it.

"Berry's never been to the abbey before," said Mark, in the car. "What about you, Calum?"

"We used to go, years ago," he said. "I can't remember much about it now—except the height of the walls. It was so strong and tall, it scared me." It wasn't the sort of thing he liked to confess, but you could tell anything to Mark.

"Yes, it used to get to me like that when I was little," said Mark. "It's not so much frightening—just big." He leaned across Calum, and pointed through the window. "Do you know whereabouts we are? The quarry's in that direction, beyond the line of trees."

"Are we near Monksmoor House?"

"Much further to the left, and further back," said Mark.

"We've already passed it, but you can't see it from the road."

"Oh." Calum was disappointed. He had been working out a theory about Myrrh and what she had been doing that night—but if the quarry was that far from Monksmoor House, it didn't make sense. Then, as the car rounded the corner, the abbey ruins came into sight and Calum forgot everything else.

In the valley, wrapped around by the misty river, towers stretched to the sky like the ragged remains of a magic castle. Towers balanced impossibly on battered twists of staircase like broken seashells, and long straight walls crumbled at the ends. *I will stand here. I will stay. Whatever rage and storms can do to me, I will stand and declare my truth,* it told him.

"Are we going *there*?" gasped Berry.

"Mist's coming into the valley," said Drew as the car stopped noisily on the gravel. He nodded a greeting to the red-faced man at the entrance hut, and the nod was all he needed to get them through the gate. Some people were already there.

"It's the Shipleys," said Calum, trying not to sound annoyed.

"Aye, they've got to check out the staging with Mark," said Drew. "If you and Berry want to explore, go ahead and lose yourselves." Then he seemed to remember something, and called to Octavia. "Octavia, you play badminton, don't you?"

No, thought Calum. *I hope not.*

Octavia shrugged, not smiling. "Sometimes," she said.

"Get together with Calum, when we're not using the barn for camping."

"I might," sighed Octavia. Clearly, it would be a great sacrifice.

"I play badminton, too," said Berry brightly.

"Oh, do you?" Octavia's tone was so disdainful that Calum wanted to hit her. She turned away, making it quite clear that she might just condescend to play Calum, but never Berry.

The mist, which had been soft and dreamlike from the road, was chilly and damp here. Calum stuffed his hands into his pockets and hunched his shoulders. When Berry jumped out at him from behind a stone pillar, pulled a face, and dashed off, he ran after her to get warm.

She led him in a dance around pillars and half-broken walls, up stone steps which led nowhere and into shells of rooms where grass grew underfoot. Dodging through an archway with moss on its top, he found himself in a little room with gravel crunching under his feet. There were stone seats carved into the wall.

It looked real. It made him imagine the monks who had sat there in their rough, tickly robes with the cowls pulled up to keep their shaven heads warm. He imagined them rubbing sandalled feet together against the cold. Perhaps Angelus had sat in this very room, angular and grinning in a habit that didn't fit him. Somewhere in the abbey were his grave and the grave of that nameless boy he had brought here in a barrow. Calum hoped they had been buried side by side.

"Calum! Calum! Calum!"

His own name rang and echoed. There was a rush of beating wings as pigeons flapped into the sky.

"Calum, come here!"

"Here!" called the echo. It was Berry's voice, and he ran to follow the sound.

"I've found their church," she called. "It's fantastic!"

He wove through the ruins until he found the right archway, and turned through it. He caught his breath.

It was a long, narrow room, with walls so high he had to crane his neck as he turned around. At the east end, empty windows arched upwards. A stone slab in the ground marked where the altar must have been. Birds' nests hung raggedly from ledges.

"It's brilliant!" he said, and his voice rang from the walls. "Brilliant!" he repeated, just to hear the echo.

"There's a staircase in here!" called Berry, and she vanished into a doorway in the wall. In a few seconds she appeared at a window above him and Calum, following, found himself in a small, bird-nested gallery above the church.

"It's bound to have bats!" said Berry.

"Suppose so," said Calum. By looking straight ahead, he could see the far-stretching moors through the gaping windows.

"Berry," he said, "I've been thinking about Myrrh and the incense box. I've got a theory, but I don't know if it works."

She probably wasn't listening. You could never tell with Berry. But he went on.

"Aunt Peachstone told me that Myrrh had stolen things before, but only to give them away. The night she ran away, a baby was born at Monksmoor House. The people at the vicarage were the first to know, including Myrrh."

Now that he was unfolding his theory, the excitement of it thrilled and warmed him. He went on, not caring if she heard him.

"It was winter — Christmas time! Myrrh heard about a new baby, so what did she want to take him? Gold, frankincense, and myrrh. And she could see how to do it. She probably thought it was what she was meant to do! What do you think, Berry?"

Berry was staring with vacant eyes across the moors, but she nodded confidently.

"It's what I would have done," she said, and Calum couldn't hold back the smile. But it faded when he scanned the moors.

"The trouble is," he said, "she was in completely the wrong place. If she was at the quarry she was nowhere near Monksmoor House. It was miles off, on her left. Maybe she was just trying to smuggle the stolen box to Sam Bagshaw."

"She was just lost," said Berry.

"How lost could she get? They were setting off guns and fireworks. She couldn't have missed Monksmoor House."

"I hope there weren't any animals about," said Berry. "They would have been frightened."

Calum gave up. If Berry was thinking in terms of animals, nothing could interest her in humans. He looked down to see James, looking very small and alone, running into the vast emptiness of the ruined church. The rest of the Shipley family followed him, then Mark and Drew.

"Try standing there, Mark," Drew was saying. "Say a few lines, and we'll see what it sounds like."

Mark stood in front of the altar slab, facing the window where Berry and Calum stood. He tilted his head back, took a deep breath, and began the speech he would say on Octave Night.

"Let this be the memorial of Angelus and the boy, as long as Beckerton stands." His loud and steady speech vibrated in the walls. "Let it be a place of warmth and welcome. Let no child ever be turned away again."

Calum looked down and saw Octavia watching Berry. He had never seen her look uneasy before, but she did now. Something had brought a tinge of pinkness to her bored, pretty face — but maybe it was just the cold, or the rosy light of the late afternoon.

Beckerton — Home of Tales and Towers.
Home of Mist and Mystery.

Seven

Over the next two weeks, the shops began to fill with Christmas decorations. The adults grumbled that it was far too early to sell them, but they bought them anyway. It was dark by the time Calum came home from school. He, Mark, and Berry carried pocket flashlights for the journey from the village to White Fox Farm.

In the village, the talk was all about the Octave. Aunt Dorcas, Mrs. Shipley, and little groups of determined women in woolly fingerless gloves cleaned and polished the church. Mrs. Percival organized trips to the abbey and concerts with supper beforehand, recitals with supper afterwards, and cozy social evenings with supper all the way through. Pat Parker arranged troughs of winter pansies around her holiday cottages and chased away inquisitive ducks who tried to eat them. Moira unloaded boxes of teabags and little pink soaps from her taxi and offered raffle tickets to anyone who stopped to help her. At the shop Mrs. Phipps, looking more worried than ever, stacked every corner with postcards, souvenir boxes of toffees, guide books, and calendars until Mr. Phipps had nowhere to sit down. He blew into the church instead and joined the cleaning team, and Alexa helped in the shop after school.

Visitors were arriving for days before the Octave was to start. Coming home on Thursday evening, Calum saw cars parked outside Mrs. Percival's guest house and smartly dressed visitors carrying in their suitcases. He walked with Berry and Mark to the farm, their strides long and purposeful in the sharp air, their breath freezing before them.

The farm shop, with its bright light and sudden warmth and Mom and Peggy smiling from the bakery window, was like another world. Mark slipped into the office, reappeared with washed hands and without his coat, and joined in serving the customers. Calum put the kettle on.

"Calum," called Peggy, "Berry's mom's getting the barn ready for the students. Take her a cup of tea when it's brewed."

Programs for the Octave were piled up beside the cash register. There was something happening every day and night of the Octave, everything from a children's fancy dress party in the village hall to a lecture on medieval abbeys at Monksmoor House. There were craft fairs, bus tours, concerts, recitals, and, of course, the final procession to the abbey. An entry for Friday night stood out from the rest in bold type.

"HOEDOWN! A warm USA welcome from the students of Midwest University who will join us at The Barn, White Fox Farm, at eight. Come to the party!"

It didn't sound very Octave-ish, and Calum couldn't see how they could hold a dance in the barn if they were camping in there. All the same, it—and the students—sounded like fun.

"They're coming a bit late, aren't they?" said Calum. "They only arrive on Friday."

"They want to stay with the other students at the Hall of Residence on Thursday," explained Peggy. "It's Thanksgiving. It's a shame, having to spend it away from their families. We'll have to make sure they feel good and welcome with us."

Calum took a tray to the barn, which now looked like an empty dormitory waiting for its furniture. By this time it had electricity, a water supply, toilets, and showers. The floor needed sweeping, and Berry's mom was cleaning the windows.

"There's a little fridge to clean and put in here, and kettles," she said. She sat on the floor and cupped her hands around her mug. "We're doing their main meals."

"It must be costing a lot to set all this up," said Calum.

"It should pay for itself," said Berry's mom. "There's nowhere else in Beckerton for cheap-and-cheerful holidays. And there are school groups, church groups, that sort of thing—they'll come here. Youngsters. This is a good place for a holiday."

"It's a good place to live," said Calum, and found that he meant it, in spite of the town's wariness and mistrust. Beckerton had Aunt Dorcas, Berry, and the Fishers. It had its history, and Angelus Lane, and the farm. And its mysteries.

Myrrh and mystery.

They swept the floor, brushed away cobwebs, carried in chairs, and cleaned the fridge. To Calum all this cleaning only seemed to stir up more dust, and most of the dust seemed to have attached itself to him by the time Peggy appeared.

"It's past time to go home! Calum, your mom's waiting. Just look at you, you need a bath." She looked down at the bag in her hands. "I'd better give this to your mom to carry, not you, you mucky article. It's your Aunt Dorcas's vegetables and the arnica cream she ordered for her rheumatism."

"It'll be rough weather, then," said Drew, arriving behind her. "If Dorcas's rheumatism's bad, it always means a cold snap. She's better than the weather folks. Give me five minutes to lock up the shop, and I'll give you a lift home."

The van bumped along the rough track to the main road. Drew carried a fan heater for Dad to repair, some teacakes, and a box of oranges which he said were too old to sell but which looked perfectly all right to Calum.

"So how are you celebrating the Octave, son?" he asked Calum. "Are you coming to the American party?"

"Definitely."

"And are you coming to the abbey, with our Mark?"

"Um—I'm certainly coming," he said cautiously. "Not exactly with Mark."

"There's no reason why you shouldn't be on the float," said Drew.

Calum looked at his feet. "Nobody's asked me to be," he said. "Mark said he mentioned it to Major Shipley, but I still haven't been asked."

"Hm," said Drew. That small sound said a great deal. Everything Drew seemed to think about Beckerton was in that "hm." Calum heard it as plainly as if Drew had explained it all slowly. Drew stood on the doorstep, looking out at the dark sky, hesitating, as if making his mind up. Then he said, "What you need to understand, son, is this. Now, get it into your head. Ready?"

"Ready," said Calum.

"The Octave of Angels is what we're famous for. Haworth has the Brontë sisters; Eyam had the plague; we've got the Octave of Angels. You think Beckerton folk love the Octave, don't you?"

"But they do! They're so proud of it, they won't let anyone new—like me—anywhere near it. They keep it to themselves because they love it so much!" said Calum.

"They don't," said Drew, with a sad, knowing face. "They don't. They hate it. At heart, they hate the Octave for all they're worth. They keep it to themselves so they can keep it under control and not face what it's really about."

"He's right," said Aunt Dorcas behind him. She walked slowly to the open door, pulling her cardigan around her. "It's true. We all pretend it isn't, but it is."

"Don't stand in the cold, Dorcas," said Drew.

"Stop fussing, Drew," she said firmly. "The Octave is about this village refusing to welcome a stranger. When the abbot started it, it wasn't a festival. It was a punishment. Do you think they liked getting a public telling-off every year?"

"But that was *then*," said Calum.

"Yes, but they still can't forget it," said Drew. "There's something strange about this place, as if they're trapped in their past and can't move on. They can't even remember Sam Bagshaw, but they look at you and whisper to each other about him!" He shook his head, and went on, "They'd rather have a Festival of Dancing Moorhags than the Octave of Angels. They still don't like strangers, even though we need the visitors. You might just get to ride on the float with Mark, because your family's always lived here, but little Berry won't—unless I can fix it for her." He smiled, and winked. "You get indoors, where it's warm, the pair of you. Goodnight."

Calum went back to Aunt Dorcas's sitting-room with her.

"If it's that bad," he said, "why have you stayed here?" She laughed, and put a hand on his shoulder.

"It's not so bad! Wherever you live you find some awkward characters, and it'll be like that until the snow catches fire. Besides," she added, easing herself stiffly into her chair, "it's my place."

"You could have moved away," he said.

"Yes, I could. But—how much do you know about me, Calum? When I married Edwin, it made sense to stay here. He was away from home, mostly, flying Spitfires . . . "

"Wow!" said Calum.

"Well, somebody had to. We rented a cottage on the far side of the bridge. It's a holiday cottage now. This was my parents' house. When Edwin was killed in action, I came back here. I was the one who stayed at home and looked after my parents when my sisters married and moved away, and I didn't mind that. I was with the people I belonged to. This is my place, where my roots are. With Edwin, I would have gone anywhere in the world. Without him, I'd rather be here. I'm glad I kept the house."

"So am I," said Calum, who felt he'd rather be here than anywhere else, too.

"Put a match to the fire," she said, and pulled a face. "I'm a creaky old woman tonight. It's going to be an early winter, and that won't be good for the Octave."

"It's only November," said Calum.

"So what? I've known snow on the Octave before. And before you say it sounds wonderful, just think of trying to get the float through snowdrifts."

"But they'd have to get through somehow! It wouldn't be the Octave, if they didn't get to the abbey!"

"Well," she admitted, "there were blizzards once, years ago, when Octavia's father was Angelus. He insisted on walking it."

"He can't have done that!"

"The major went with him, of course, and one or two other tough old warriors. I believe they took a shortcut across the moors and stayed somewhere overnight."

"*Octavia's* father?"

"He doesn't seem to you like the type, does he? That'll teach you to jump to conclusions about people. Shouldn't you be doing some homework, or helping to get tea ready, or

69

something?"

He got up to go, still thinking about what she'd said.

"Are there many shortcuts across the moor?" he asked.

She looked up sharply. "For those who know their way, yes. But don't you try it, and never go on the moors alone. I'm not talking about moorhags and such, I'm talking about just plain getting lost and still being lost after dark. If you want to go exploring, go with Drew, or Mark, or somebody else who really knows their way around. Don't try it alone."

"No chance!" said Calum. He went to the kitchen, where the dresser was piled high with oranges.

"Snow for the Octave?" his mother was saying. "Not until . . . "

"The snow catches fire?" grinned his father, and winked at Calum. "But it can't, can it, if there isn't any snow. And there won't be."

φ   φ   φ

At his window that night, watching the lights of faraway farms, Calum thought of more postcards.

Beckerton — Home of the Octavia of Shipley.
       Pity, but somebody has to have her.

Beckerton — Home of the Hoedown.
       The Hoedown of Angels.

70

Eight

At first, it didn't snow. It rained, beginning with a steady drizzle as the church filled up for the Octave service. Aunt Dorcas had warned Calum to be there early to be sure of getting a seat, so they walked down through a fine mist of rain that shimmered in the street lamps and in the bright white floodlights in the churchyard. Fresh flowers lay on Myrrh's grave.

The church was nearly full. The central pews were filled with visitors in smart winter jackets, and most of the village came, latecomers filling up the front pews where nobody else liked to sit. The visitors, waiting for the service to begin, gazed around at the frescoes and whispered, but Calum felt the place in those pictures where Myrrh should have been as if it reached out and touched him. The gold incense box stood on the altar, open, filled with darkly-colored grains of resin. There was a service with a specially written hymn about Angelus, and a sermon during which Calum added and subtracted the numbers on the hymn board. Afterwards there was mulled wine in the village hall.

"Cheap red plonk and a bit of cinnamon," said Alexa. "I know, I helped to make it. I'm going home."

As Octave week went on, Calum pretended not to feel disappointed. It was like any other week. There were flags outside the houses, and banners flapped across the street proclaiming, "The Octave of Angels, November 23 - 30." But that was all the difference it made. He went to school and came home as usual. Most of the evening events were aimed at adults, and particularly at the visitors. Still, there was the procession to look forward to and, before that, the Americans.

On Thursday, coming home on the bus, Calum and Mark could see the grey cloud over Beckerton before they drove into it. Thin wet slashes appeared on the windows and became waterfalls. Water bounced from the road, it sprayed from the wheels, it swished down as they stepped from the bus and drenched them as they pulled their coats over their heads and ran home through puddles.

"Come home with me!" yelled Calum to Mark and Berry, and they didn't argue. They stood breathless in the hall with rain running down their faces and Aunt Dorcas gasping and tutting at them.

"Off with those wet boots! Calum! Towels! I've just lit the fire. Come in, come in. Don't stand there dripping. Come and get dry. I'll get you all a hot drink."

"It's all right, Mrs. Beeston," began Mark, "there's no need . . ."

"Do as you're told!" she ushered them to the hearth and

towelled vigorously at Berry's hair. "Berry, phone home, let your mom know where you are."

"I'll phone the shop," said Mark. "She'll be there. Mom or Dad might be able to pick us up."

"Tell them not to come till you've had some hot chocolate," said Aunt Dorcas.

"Wow might worry about me," gasped Berry, through chattering teeth. "He knows when I get home. He watches for me." Pink toes peeped through her socks as she wriggled out of her boots, and she peeled off the damp socks and spread them in front of the fire. "Wow likes my socks. He carries them to his basket when I'm not there."

"We'll soon get you home, Strawberry," said Mark, then interrupted himself to speak into the phone. There was some one-sided conversation, then he put it down.

"Dad'll be here in half an hour or so. With any luck, we might not get to school tomorrow. We've had flood warnings."

"Great!" said Berry.

"It won't look so good for the Octave," he said. "Not if the road to the abbey gets flooded with the water running off the moors."

It wasn't what Calum wanted to hear. "It isn't going to go on raining, is it, Aunt Dorcas?" he said. "You said it would turn cold."

"Yes," she said, "it will. I can feel it. I do hope your Americans get here."

✠   ✠   ✠

The school bus did get through on Friday, and so did the Americans. The rain had stopped, but the sudden chill Aunt Dorcas had predicted was already in the air. Calum was at the barn door with Mark and Peggy when a mud-splashed minibus jerked and squeaked to a stop beside them. There was a banging of doors, some shouts and laughter, and the American students tumbled out of the bus and into the barn. A tall, dark-haired young man appeared in the doorway with a rolled-up sleeping bag under his arm.

"Hi, Peggy! I remember you. I'm Nick," he announced. When Peggy introduced him to Mark and Calum, he smiled as if they were old friends. "Calum's a Scotch name, isn't it? You Scotch?"

"No, but my dad's family was, a long way back."

"Mine, too. A very long way back." He looked around the barn as if he wanted to buy it, and nodded. "Wow, this is neat. Real neat. Come and meet the guys."

There were so many of them, Calum knew he wouldn't figure out who was who before they went home again. But somebody unloaded a football from the bus and suddenly they were all playing five-a-side, or three- or four-a-side depending on who was playing and who was unloading the van and who'd gone off to explore. When all the backpacks and sleeping bags and cardboard boxes and crates had been unloaded the score was twelve-all, and it was impossible to play any more without hitting something. By then, Calum knew that the tall girl with the braids was Melanie, the short round guy who walked like one of those wobbly toy clowns

74

was Tom, and Nick was a good person to have on your team. Tom carried a whistle around his neck and blew a long, loud shriek.

"OK, guys," he said, "let's get our act together." Then there was a very efficient fetching and carrying while bags and baggage were pushed out of the way and the sound system was set up, and Peggy came in to say that they could set the tables in the shop if they wanted to, and were they all warm enough, and there was hot soup waiting for them. Walking over to the shop, they turned up their collars and hunched their shoulders against the cold.

"It must be warmer than this in Minnesota," said Calum, but Nick shook his head.

"We have real winters back home. Snowdrifts. Will it snow here?"

"My Aunt Dorcas says it will," said Calum, "and she's usually right."

"She's always right," said Peggy, "and Berry's just gone past with her dog. He's holding his head up and sniffing the air to smell the changes. We don't often have snow for the Octave, but this year I think we will."

"Not enough to spoil the Octave?" asked Calum.

"Of course not, love," she said, and passed him a mug of soup. "I'm looking forward to this party."

"Have you ever had pumpkin pie?" said Melanie. "We've got a lot left over from Thanksgiving." There were a few grins and giggles from the students. "Not everyone likes it."

"We've got trail mix to use up, too," said Nick. "It's kind of like rabbit food, but it's traditional. We bought way too much. We didn't really know how much to get. None of us have ever been away from home for Thanksgiving before."

"What's your Thanksgiving about?" asked Calum. "Is it a bit like Christmas?"

"It's a family thing," said Tom. "It's called Thanksgiving because it celebrates the Pilgrims bringing in their first harvest. The local Native Americans taught them about which crops they could grow, or they would never have made it through their first year. So at Thanksgiving the Native Americans and the Pilgrims all sat down to eat together, the locals and the newcomers."

"The Octave should be like that," said Calum.

"I thought it was," said Nick. "This soup is just wonderful, Peggy. Even better than my mom's."

"Is it okay if we set off a few fireworks?" asked Tom. "We have some of those left over, also."

"Somebody warn Berry, for goodness' sake," said Mark.

"We'd enjoy fireworks," said Peggy. "It's going to be a right good evening."

It was. Peggy called it a right good evening, Nick called it a real good hoedown, Mrs. Shipley said it was jolly good fun, and Calum's dad said he supposed it was better than a slap in the face with a wet fish. Calum decided that, if he got fed up with Beckerton, he'd go and work for Drew until he'd saved up enough money to go to college in Minnesota. Everybody got up and danced, and it didn't matter that nobody had heard of any of the dances because they learned as they went along. If you made mistakes, nobody minded, and as they danced the students clapped and shouted and whooped, until all the Beckerton people were shouting and clapping and whooping, too. All, that is, except Aunt Dorcas, who enjoyed the fun from a chair where she sat clapping and beating her foot on the floor, and a few locals who huddled in a corner. Mrs. Percival said that it was "not very Beckerton," and Moira pointed out that it was all good fun but it was nothing to do with the Octave, and she'd like to bet Drew Fisher wasn't charging the students enough for the barn. Mark, who had gone to the shop for more drinks, came in and thudded a heavy crate on to a table.

"It's perishing out there," he said, his voice breathless with cold. "It's freezing hard. I hate to break up the party, but it might be an idea if the people who came by car got ready to go home."

"Don't you salt and sand the roads?" asked Tom.

"Not much up here," said Mark. "If the town sand truck gets up here, it's usually too late."

"Don't make a fuss about a little touch of ice," said Mrs. Shipley. But she went outside and came back with her nose and cheeks pink.

"Mark's right," she said. She tapped a teaspoon on a cup, and Tom blew his whistle. The chatter died down.

"Due to the weather," announced Mrs. Shipley, "I think the party will have to end now. The roads will be treacherous before long."

"We only have to get as far as the village," said someone.

"It's still not a good idea to drive on sheets of ice," said Drew. "You could always walk home and leave your cars here, but I wouldn't recommend falling down, either."

"It's not looking good for tomorrow night," said Berry's mom, and there was a worried murmur.

"Snow's forecast," said Drew.

"We will all meet in the village hall at six tomorrow," announced Major Shipley. "Then we can see what the conditions are like, and decide what we're going to do."

"We can't cancel the Octave!" complained Octavia.

"We can't control the weather, either," said her grandfather, and turned with a smile to Aunt Dorcas. "Dorcas, there was one year when it was cancelled, wasn't there?"

"There was, yes," she said. "Our splendid Angelus and his escort managed to get to the abbey, but there was no procession. And it wasn't the end of the world, you know. The church didn't fall down. The ducks didn't abandon the pond. Nobody died."

But it has to happen, thought Calum, because I can't bear it not to. My first winter in Beckerton, there has to be the Octave of Angels, and it has to be done properly.

"I don't mind walking it," said Mark.

"Is that dangerous?" asked Nick, shifting the chewing gum in his mouth.

Mark shrugged. "Only if you meet a moorhag."

"I could come with you," volunteered Nick, but Mrs. Shipley stepped in quickly and said that it wouldn't be necessary, thank you very much. Soon everyone was putting on boots and scarves and filing outside, gasping at how cold it was, and warning each other not to slip.

Calum stayed to help clean up. By the time the dishes were washed and the students were unfolding their blankets and sleeping bags, Calum was discovering what it was to be really tired and Drew was jingling the keys of the Land Rover.

"I'll take you home now," he said. "The Land Rover's a bit beat-up but it's built for tough conditions."

Calum went to the door and stood there, hushed and startled. A shiver of cold and astonishment tingled down his back. White flakes of snow descended through the night air, silent as magic.

✠   ✠   ✠

Excitement and worry meant that he slept restlessly. He slipped in and out of dreams of snow and moorhags and a girl disappearing into the moors. Sometimes it was Myrrh, and sometimes she turned into Berry. Waking, he was aware of muffled stillness. He got up, wrapped his robe tightly around himself, and padded to the window.

Snow had never looked so perfect, nor so astonishing. Calum looked down on it like an eagle from a crag. It enfolded the rise and fall of the moors like a shawl. It sparkled from the rooftops. It laced the fences and sat on the gateposts like fur. Softly, thickly, it lay across the garden, pitted with sparrow prints. From the eaves above his window hung a row of jagged icicles. Children on the green, bright in hats and mittens, were building snowmen.

He dressed quickly, and went downstairs. The small figure of Aunt Dorcas, bundled up in her coat and boots, was putting bread on the bird table.

"Here he is, the Sleeping Beauty," remarked his father. "You're missing the snow. I've never seen anything like it, not in November."

"I suppose nobody told the snow it's November," said Aunt Dorcas, coming in from the garden. She stamped her boots on the mat and left a scattering of snow. "It's very nice to look at, Calum, but it's a shame about the Octave."

He'd already thought about that. He couldn't hope for two really good things to happen at the same time, the snow and the Octave. It was truly wonderful snow for sledding and snowballs and going out to get frozen and damp, knowing you could come in and get warm again. Perfect snow. But he hadn't been looking forward to the snow. He'd been looking forward to the procession and the abbey.

Aunt Dorcas put a hand on his shoulder as she kicked off her boots. "There's a sled in the shed. It'll need a wash down, but I'm sure you and Berry can do that. I'm afraid it's not a question of whether we'll have the procession tonight. It's a question of what we'll do instead."

Calum and Berry spent most of the day sledding down a hill at the farm, with the students. Peggy brought out a sled, too, and Melanie improvised something with crates and tea-trays. Wow liked sitting on sleds until they started moving, when he panicked, jumped off, and ran behind, barking. Everyone threw snowballs for him, and sometimes he was fast enough to catch them and bite into them as they disintegrated. More often they landed in the drifts, where he snuffled about hunting for them. Berry tried to say he was shovelling snow, but she was too cold to manage the words.

"He's snovelling!" she stammered. "Look, snow snovelling!"

"Great," said Nick. "He can clear the roads to the abbey for us."

"It's only a little bit of snow," said Melanie. "We get much more than this at home. Why should it stop the procession?"

"Because we're at the back end of beyond on a moor, and the roads don't get cleared," said Nick, a bit breathlessly as he pulled a sled uphill. "This is England, okay?"

⊕ ⊕ ⊕

Everyone who had anything to do with the Octave met in the village hall that evening. The Shipleys had provided mulled wine and soft drinks, and Calum was given the job of collecting empty glasses. Mrs. Percival and Pat Parker sat in a corner and discussed whether to give discounts if their visitors were snowbound and had to stay for an extra night. The older people talked about processions they remembered from the past in rain, hail, and ice, but they all agreed they had never known a year like this.

A few people were complaining that the vicar wasn't there, but Peggy pointed out that the vicar had three parishes to look after and was snowed up in one of them.

"Drew's the churchwarden," she said. "He'll handle

everything."

Apart from the others, in a little group around the front of the stage, stood Drew, the Shipleys, and Aunt Dorcas. Mark knelt on the stage with a map spread out beside him. There was much discussion and pointing to the map, and consulting Drew, and looking at the map again. Calum heard someone saying, "You don't have to, Mark. It doesn't matter that much."

"It matters to me," said Mark.

Hanging from a coathanger on a door was Mark's costume, a plain, long sleeved tunic made of something that looked like sacks and a coarse shirt to wear underneath it. When he saw it, Calum felt reassured. Something was going to happen if Mark's costume was hanging up, ready to be worn. Mark himself sat quietly on the stage, as if he'd said all he had to say.

Major Shipley banged the stage to call for silence. The chatter died away.

"I regret to have to tell you," he said, "that there is no question of the float, or any other vehicle, getting to the abbey tonight. Last week's heavy rain means that there is a layer of ice under the snow, so roads are treacherous. Instead we shall have a procession, on foot, around the village." There was a murmur of approval. "We will start from here, walk up Church Lane, along The Rise, around the green, and back to the church. Mark will say his speech there, instead of at the abbey."

"As well as," said Mark.

"Then we'll all come back here for a . . . a social evening," went on Major Shipley. "I'm sure we can manage some sort of a party at short notice. Meanwhile, Mark . . . ," he turned and looked at Mark. "Mark, with an escort, intends to walk over the moors to the abbey. We've told him he doesn't have to do it, but he feels it's important."

"It's not *that* important, surely?" said Calum's mother.

"It is to me," said Mark. "And it is to the village, because of what the Octave is really about."

"We've planned a route," said Drew. "It'll take us near Monksmoor House, so we can shelter there if we have to. We'll keep in touch by mobile phone, if the signal's any good. Failing that, we can phone from Monksmoor House or the abbey. We're idiots to do this, so I'm trying to make the plan idiot-proof."

"And if it isn't?" asked Major Shipley.

Mark shrugged. "We'll be lost idiots," he said.

"I'll get lost with you," said Octavia's father. "Three idiots are safer than two, and I've done it before."

From the back of the hall came a clear voice with an American twang. "You want any more volunteers?"

"That won't be necessary, thank you," replied the major crisply.

"Thanks all the same, Nick," said Mark, and grinned towards the back of the hall. "Perhaps you could form a search party if we don't get in touch?"

"Sure." As Mark jumped down from the stage and took his costume from its hanger, Calum caught his arm.

"Can I come with you to the abbey?" he asked.

"Sorry, son," said Drew from behind him. "No chance. The snow would be over the tops of your boots. It'll be real hard going over the moors tonight. I wouldn't have done it myself, but Mark's being pig-headed about it."

"That's the point about the Octave," said Mark. "It isn't meant to be easy. Dad, the incense box should be carried around the village in the procession. Has anyone been chosen to do that?"

A look passed between father and son.

"Yes," said Drew. "Calum's doing it. Hasn't anyone told you, Calum? We'll go and get it while Mark changes into his frock, or whatever it's meant to be. Mind, Calum, it's precious, so if you fall on the ice make sure you're the one who gets a bruising, not the box."

The box had been dropped before, and it was still in one piece. Myrrh must have held on tightly to it, even in her last moments. And now he would carry it around the village on the final night of the Octave of Angels. He was still tasting the joy when Nick came to speak to Drew.

"I hope we caused no offense, offering to help out tonight," said Nick. "Tom just reminded me, we still have fireworks from last night. Rockets and stuff. Do you want to take them with you? If you set them off at intervals, we'll be able to see where you are."

"Good thinking!" said Drew. "And set some off at the farm, will you? It'll help us to keep our bearings."

It occurred to Calum that there was something they ought

to remember about fireworks. But there was the procession to think about, and soon he was hurrying to the church with Drew.

On its shelf lay the box, gleaming with gold and fragrant with incense. Calum lifted it down, feeling that it was as if he placed his hands over Myrrh's. On one corner, the inlay was damaged. Carrying it away, he felt the eyes of the Beckerton villagers, watching him from the painted walls.

Beckerton — Home of Ice and Incense.
Beckerton Moor. Home of — what?
                    poachers?
                    moorhags?

Home of whatever lay between Beckerton and the abbey.
For Myrrh, it had been death.
Calum shivered.

Nine

As the crowd gathered at the church door, Calum saw that many of them had put on medieval costumes. Octavia Shipley wore a long tunic and cloak and carried a lantern. Mark appeared, no longer looking like Mark in the layers of rough tunics. A pair of huge boots bulged out under the hem.

"Yes," said Mark, "and I've got a sweater and two pairs of socks underneath all this, too. I had to borrow a pair of Dad's boots to get over them. Are you warm enough, kid?"

Calum nodded and gave the box to Mark until he had pulled his padded gloves on. He could hear somebody asking whether it was wise to take the box from the church and who had given permission.

"The churchwarden gave permission," said Drew. "That's me." At the door stood a wooden cart like a large and hefty crate on wheels, with a rope attached to one end.

"Angelus had a cart," Mark reminded Calum, "so I have to drag this thing around the village. Pity he didn't go around with a sled."

"I'm sure the box would be safer in the cart," said Mr. Shipley.

"Not with our Mark pulling it," said Drew. Then Major Shipley called for quiet. Drew led a prayer. Heads were bowed, and the words rang into solemn silence.

"Amen," said everyone.

"Now," whispered Mark, and they stepped forward together into the bite of the sharp air.

The snow that had looked stunning in daylight was magical by night, like a dangerous magic that could trap you and hold you in its darkness. Boots crunched and squeaked in the snow; the cart rumbled and creaked. Frosty air nipped Calum's ears. Stride for stride, he stayed level with Mark. Somewhere, a fox barked. From lighted upstairs windows, people looked down to watch them. Behind Calum, the church choir sent their song spinning into the icy air. Occasionally there was a slither and bump from behind them as someone fell down.

"Don't look around," said Mark, "or you'll go down, too." They paused now and again for the stragglers in the procession to catch up. Mark and Calum led the way along the middle of the road where the snow was lightest, but when they stopped Calum saw that most of the followers were walking on the edge of the pavement where they could hang on to walls and gateposts. Alexa, who had pretended not to be interested, was struggling along with a bright smile on her face and Aunt Dorcas on her arm.

"You should go home, auntie, if you're getting cold," said

Calum's father.

"Cheek!" said Aunt Dorcas, and went on shuffling through the snow and holding tightly to Alexa. Mark laughed.

"She's a tough old bird, your Aunt Dorcas," he said. "Not far now."

Past the village green with its sinking footprints. Up the church path, where Mark left the cart. Into the church, and down the aisle to the steps.

"Stop and turn around here," said Mark. The followers huddled in and stood with puddles of melting snow forming around their boots. Mark began his speech. In the tiny village church it wasn't as powerful and dramatic as it had been when he rehearsed it in the abbey, but the words were spoken and Calum, holding the box, was part of it.

There was a prayer and a blessing. People began to scurry out to the party in the hall. *Is that it?* thought Calum as he returned the box to its place. Peggy and some of the students came to meet them.

"That was real neat," said Nick. "Can we come to see you off, Mark?"

"You're absolutely determined to do this, are you, Mark?" asked Peggy. Mark just grinned.

"I'll be all right, Mom. I won't let the moorhags get me. Then again, they might get Dad."

"You'll not have a grain of sense till the snow catches fire, not between the pair of you," said Peggy. "I suppose you're going too, are you, Calum?"

"And me!" said Berry, who had been hidden in the press of

students. So, with students and the Fishers and all the other hangers-on and see-ers-off, Calum was never quite sure how many of them went to White Fox Farm that night.

✠ ✠ ✠

"I'm not hiking over the moors in a dress," said Mark, when they got there. "I'll take it with me and change at the abbey." In fact, all three walkers looked like explorers at the North Pole by the time Calum and the others waved them off at the edge of the road. When the last of their lights had disappeared, Calum reluctantly turned his back on the dark moor.

"What d'you think, Mel?" Nick was saying. "Back to the party?"

"Sure," she said, and put an arm around Berry. "You coming with us, Berry?"

"No th-thanks," said Berry, stammering with cold and shuffling her hands into her sleeves for warmth. "I'm going home to Wow."

"I'll see you home, Berry," said Peggy, though Berry was already stamping along ahead of her. "The rest of you go on to the party. I'll join you later."

So Calum went to the party, which turned out to be a happy mess of music, dancing, silly games, and people taking turns to sing, play an instrument, or — in Tom's case — juggle. It didn't have much to do with the Octave, but it was fun. Octavia's mother tried to get her to do the dances she had learned for her ballet exam, and Octavia refused and swept out with her nose in the air.

But all the time Calum's heart and mind were somewhere else. He was out on the bare, frozen moor with Mark, fighting their way through to the abbey for the sake of the Octave of Angels. He went outside, knowing he'd feel nearer to them there. The snow blew lightly into his face with a sharp edge on the wind as he leaned his arms against the churchyard wall. The spire nudged the clouds. The stars were hiding.

Looking down at the glistening snow he saw that Myrrh's grave was almost hidden, but there were fresh flowers on it. He wished he knew who put them there. It was another of Beckerton's secrets. Shadows and secrets, things half-understood, half-seen, like the dim shape of Myrrh's grave.

A voice cried out in the icy air. It was a child's voice. A girl's voice, high and distressed and so full of pain that it chilled Calum to hear it. It came again, a heart-breaking scream that called his name.

"Calum! Calum!"

A child came lurching through the snow towards him. Wild hair straggled around her face, and she carried something in her hand.

He wanted to back away. He couldn't move. Then, as she came nearer, a surge of relief washed through him.

"Berry!" He hoped he didn't sound angry but he was, angry with her for scaring him and with himself for being scared. "What are you playing at?"

She stumbled nearer, and he forgot his anger when he saw her face. Her eyes, puffy with crying, were filling with tears again.

"I've lost Wow!" Her mouth began to stretch and distort with crying. "He ran off! He could be anywhere!"

"When?" He took her by the shoulders. "What direction? Have you called for him?"

As he spoke he heard a man's voice, somewhere on the far side of the church, yelling, "WOW! *WOW!*" If Berry hadn't been worried half out of her senses, it would have been funny.

"We've looked everywhere," she sniffed. "That's my dad, calling for him. He'd let him out into the garden to pee, and then somebody set off a firework and Wow got scared and jumped the fence and bolted!"

The students. They were setting off fireworks to help the walkers keep their bearings. And Wow had been outside.

"He'll be lost on the moor somewhere, trying to get home, and it's freezing!" She rubbed her sleeve across her eyes, pulled a raggy tissue from her sleeve and blew her nose. "He'll be crying for me, and I'm not there!"

There was a sound of boots crunching and slithering on the snow, and her father appeared with a flashlight in his hand.

"It's no good, love," he said. "Come on home. I'll go out at first light, I promise. He'll come to no harm before then. If he's got any sense he'll find somewhere to shelter and curl up for the night."

"What if he's hurt? He could be lying somewhere, bleeding or hurting or *anything*," wept Berry.

"Yes, and we'll all end up lying somewhere hurting if we go out on a night like this," he said grimly. "Come on, love.

Home."

She wiped her face again, gulped, and nodded. Then she seemed to think again.

"I'd rather go to the party," she said.

To Calum, this was the oddest thing she could have come out with. Go to a party, when she was sobbing her heart out for a missing dog? But her father seemed relieved.

"Good idea, love. It'll take your mind off things. Go and have fun. I'll pick you up later."

He walked away across the snow. Calum and Berry tramped to the hall, heads down, neither of them speaking. A firework banged into the sky and Berry sobbed quietly.

At the party, she suddenly brightened up. Calum was enjoying the games, but he looked around now and again to see where she was. She was always clasping the arm of one or another of the students and beaming up into their faces as she chatted to them. He'd never seen her so affectionate towards anything with less than four legs. Perhaps she'd taken a fancy to Nick or one of the others. It was much later when he looked around and couldn't see her at all. Looking for her, he found Melanie making fruit punch in the kitchen.

"Have you seen Berry?" he asked.

"I think she's around somewhere," said Melanie. "I guess she's still trying to recruit guys for her search party."

Oh, no, thought Calum, *she isn't, is she?* "What search party?" he asked.

"Did you know her dog ran off . . . ? She was trying to coax Nick into going to look for him. Nick reckoned she had no chance of finding him tonight, and next time I saw her she was trying to get to Tom. Is something wrong?"

"She's missing. I think she's gone by herself," he said. "She couldn't get anyone to help her look for the dog, so she's gone alone."

The door clicked open, and Octavia came in. She saw Calum and wrinkled her nose.

"Have you seen Berry?" he demanded. "It's very important."

"*Very* important, Octavia," added Melanie. "She may be lost."

"I saw her putting her coat on," she said. "It was when we were getting into teams for that game."

Melanie looked at her watch. "How far could she get in ten minutes?"

"She probably knows all the short cuts," said Calum.

Melanie put down the cartons of fruit juice. "OK, tell you what we do," she said. "The van's outside; it's pretty good on bad roads. I'll take you as far as the turning to the farm, and hope we catch up with her. If not, we come back here and organize a search party to find her. Octavia, can you make the punch? You only need to—"

"I'll get my boots. I'm coming with you," said Octavia. Calum didn't want her to, but there was no time to argue. Melanie drove slowly out of the village as snowflakes whirled eerily in and out of the headlights. No sign of Berry.

"The mist will come in soon," said Octavia. "It always does, very quickly, when it's like this." She didn't say, "I'm the expert on these moors," but Calum could hear it in her voice.

"Okay, so don't wander off," ordered Melanie, parking the van. She took a flashlight as they got out. "Take a deep breath, and after a count of three, yell."

They shouted and shouted again, louder and higher until Calum's throat hurt. Nobody answered. Their voices vanished into the snow.

"Okay, now we get a search party," said Melanie promptly. "We'll get back and get organized."

"I'll wait here," said Calum, "in case Berry or the dog turn up."

"That works," said Melanie. "Keep the flashlight."

"I'll stay, too," said Octavia. "It's safer with two."

"Safer than what?" asked Calum, but Melanie was already in the van. He and Octavia waited, stamping their feet against the cold, turning the flashlight in all directions.

"This is no good," said Octavia presently. "We could grow old and die waiting for Melanie. We'll go ahead."

"No!" said Calum. "We need more than two of us, and we need to be organized. Small groups going in different directions, signals, that sort of thing." He couldn't resist adding, "You know so much about the moors, you must know that."

She stepped nearer and glared into his face.

"Yes, I do know, poacher, and I'm the only one of you who knows *anything* about these moors. Probably not as much as the famous Samuel Bagshaw, but enough, and I'm going to look for stupid Berry and her thick mangy dog." Pulling her

94

collar up she turned away, but Calum grabbed her arm.

"Why are you so worried about Berry?" he demanded. "You've done nothing but put her down since I've been here, and now you want to risk your neck to find her!"

"I don't like her, if that's what you mean," she snapped back. "I think she's a total waste of space, but so what? I'm not a monster. I don't like your precious raspberry or bilberry or whatever she thinks she is, but I won't leave her to freeze on the moors, even if you will. You're her friend. If you're too wet to come with me you can stay here and wait for nice Auntie Melanie." She was hunting through her pockets as she spoke, and pulled out a pocket flashlight. "I'll use this. I'll leave you the big one in case you're frightened."

She turned to go, but Calum grabbed at her arm and held her back. With his free hand he shaded his face against the snow blowing in his eyes.

"You're not interested in Berry," he said. "You just want to do everything your own way, and you can't bear Melanie telling you what to do. What do you think you are, the Queen of Beckerton?"

"What does it matter?" she wrenched her arm away. "It's your precious little friend who'll get rescued!"

"And how many people will have to risk their necks coming out after you, if you get lost?" he demanded.

"Oh, you're pathetic! I'm going!" She strode away powerfully through the snow, not looking back.

She's only doing it to be a hero, thought Calum. But if she was determined to go, he couldn't leave her to take the risks alone.

With all Aunt Dorcas's warnings replaying in his head he ran after her, lifting his feet high through the heaviness of the drifts. Octavia gave a scowl and a shrug to show she knew he was there.

"Keep shouting," said Calum.

They cupped their hands and yelled, but they heard nothing. Octavia took a guess at where the path was, but Calum pointed out that while Berry might stick to a path, Wow wouldn't. They stopped and shouted, calling in all directions, turning around and around. Sometimes the light showed trees ruffled with snow or rocks lapped around with drifts, but more often it showed only a mysterious circle of hazy light with the flakes falling slowly through the flashlight's glow.

"It's like Narnia!" exclaimed Octavia.

Typical! thought Calum. Snow was dripping from his hair into his eyes and his toes stung with cold. She was right, though—he turned slowly, guiding the flashlight's beam in a sweeping circle, lighting up the silent descent of snow, mysterious and beautiful.

"Which way now?" he said.

Octavia took the flashlight and swung it in an arc. "Head to that clump of trees," she said. "That's just off the track."

They trudged on, fingers bitten with cold, snow on their eyelashes. Stop, call, listen. Calum thought of Melanie and the search party arriving and finding them gone, but there was nothing he could do about that now. He hoped they'd hear them shouting, or see the flashlight's beam, or . . . or something. Sooner or later they'd all be home, drying out their wet clothes and laughing about this. At least they couldn't get much colder.

A firework exploded far behind them. They turned, but through the snow it was impossible to trace the fall of glowing sparks.

"Sounds like that sort of direction," said Calum, pointing with a shivering hand. There was an answering bang from somewhere beyond them. "If that first firework was at the farm, the second one must have been a response from the walkers."

"If it hadn't been for your American friends and their fireworks, this wouldn't have happened," muttered Octavia.

"Oh, come on! What have you got against the Americans? Come to that, what have you got against everybody?"

"You don't get it, do you?" Octavia stamped on through the snow. "The Octave is the Octave. It's beautiful, and special, and ancient, and it's *ours*. We don't need new people coming in and taking over and thinking they know all about it. We don't need a bunch of noisy students making it an excuse for a party. It'll get ruined, just like Christmas gets ruined every year with silly songs and ads for Barbie dolls. I don't suppose you have a clue what I mean, have you?"

"I know." It was so cold, speech was difficult, and Calum struggled. "I know exactly what you mean, and that's why I really wanted to be part of the Octave. But you won't do any good by being so prickly about it."

"Oh, you're just the poa—" she began, and stopped, as if

97

she regretted it. They trudged on without saying anything, then Octavia shrieked.

"What is it?" demanded Calum. Octavia's hands were pressed to her face and her eyes stared with fright. Swinging the light ahead of them, Calum could see only a bare winter tree. Its long, delicate branches swung like the arms of a spectral witch.

"It was right across my face," muttered Octavia with chattering teeth. She stepped back, looking at the tree in the light of the flashlight. "Stupid tree!" she snapped and kicked the tree so viciously that Calum knew she had been truly frightened.

"Did you think it was a moorhag?" he said, and she glared at him.

"It's time we shouted again," she snapped, "if we're ever going to find your stupid Berry and her stupid, stupid dog. She shouldn't be allowed out on her own."

They called, their throats aching in the cold, but there was still no answer. Calum, who hadn't expected one, wondered how far and how long they'd walked.

"Whereabouts *are* we?" he asked.

There was a long silence, like a grey shadow creeping over him. At last, in a small and shaky voice she said, "I don't know."

She stood with her head down. Calum, trying to work out what to do next, found his mind had become as blank as the darkness all around them. Then, just as he felt he was as cold as he could ever be, his spine turned to needles of ice inside him.

A sound reached them across the moors. A high, mournful voice, wailing and keening in the enfolding dark.

Ten

Even though he knew that moorhags could not exist, white fear held Calum. In the pale light, Octavia's face was fixed and staring.

The keening died away. Calum told himself again that there were no such things as moorhags. Whatever it was, it couldn't be that.

It came again, louder and desperate with pain and sorrow. As it faded it was weak, pleading, and heartbreaking. It ended with a miserable yap. Calum and Octavia broke into wild, relieved laughter, and a welcome heat came to Calum's face.

"We've found Wow!" he said, laughing, and didn't admit that he'd taken the voice for a moorhag. Neither did Octavia. The dog howled again, and they struggled forward, lifting the flashlights to cast the light ahead of them.

"Wow!" yelled Calum. "Wow! It's all right, we're coming! You'll be all right!" The howling grew louder, with short, urgent barks.

"I can see prints," called Octavia. "Over to our right—not

pawprints. Feet. Somebody's been here . . . "

"Sh!" said Calum, and stopped. Amidst the crying of the dog another voice spoke in the dark, low and struggling to speak. "Calum!"

"Berry!" Calum stumbled forward into the dark drifts. Berry spoke again, eerie and invisible, from somewhere beyond him.

"Don't, Calum! Stop! It's—"

The ground gave way beneath his feet. He was slipping, not into snow, but into emptiness.

There were seconds of wild terror, feet flailing, hands scrabbling. As the flashlight tumbled out of reach he grabbed at the ground above him, found icy grass and earth to cling to, and, with a cold sweat of relief, found his feet were touching the ground.

"Don't move," said Berry. Beneath him, her voice was low and hampered by cold.

"I can't," muttered Calum through clenched teeth. He pressed his fingers into the frozen earth above him. "I can't move. I don't know what's around me."

A light shone from somewhere beneath him—Berry must have picked up his flashlight. Octavia's small light shone weakly down.

"It's the quarry," whispered Berry.

"It can't be," said Octavia. "We haven't come as far as . . . oh, it is! We've walked miles! Calum . . . "

"Just don't tell me again not to move," he muttered.

"Actually, Calum, I think you should," said Octavia. "No,

listen — I can see from here. Berry and the dog are curled up at the bottom of the cliff beneath you. You're on a ledge, but it's not far down to where she is. This must be the shallow side of the quarry. If you edge your way along and climb down, you might be able to reach her."

"Won't it be a lot easier if we both just get hold of the dog and climb out?" said Calum.

"I can't," said Berry, and Calum could hear her fighting the threat of tears. "I put my hand down when I fell, and it really hurts. I got a bit bruised, too. And Wow keeps crying. I think he's injured. And anyway, I'm not getting out without him, and he can't climb, and . . . , " then her voice became high and wobbly, and there was a choked little sob.

"I'm coming down, Berry," he said.

"And I'm going for help," said Octavia. "I'll follow our footprints back, and I'll keep shouting. The search party should be there somewhere."

"Wait until I get down to where Berry is," said Calum, adjusting the grip of his fingers as the padded gloves slipped on the slithery grass. "Octavia, pull my gloves off for me, I can't hold on with them."

He felt her chilled fingers holding tightly to one wrist at a time to keep him from falling as she pulled off his gloves. The cold of the grass ran into his arms.

"Shuffle along to your right," said Octavia. "Keep going."

It was easy for her to say. Calum, his palms pressed against the cliff face, edged sideways. It seemed that the ledge was getting wider. He kept his face turned to the side, the cliff scraping his skin. He wouldn't look down.

"Now kneel on the ledge," said Octavia.

"What?"

"Trust me, you can do it, you've got room. Then climb down."

Bracing himself against the rock, he lowered himself on to one knee, then two. The snow had drifted to this end of the ledge. It seeped through to his skin, and his feet hung over the edge.

"Now climb down as far as you can, holding on to the ledge. Then jump," ordered Octavia.

He was concentrating too hard to be frightened. He lowered himself over the ledge, groping for toeholds, hanging on with stinging fingers to the ledge.

"You're nearly there," said Octavia.

He let go. With a slither and a bump, he landed in soft snow and tried to see where he was.

"Berry?" he said.

"I'm here," she said from somewhere near him.

"To your right, in the angle of the rock," said Octavia. "I think it's a bit more sheltered in there." A faint beam of light guided him until he found them.

A sharp right-angled corner in the rock face gave a little shelter from the snow and wind. In the dim light Calum could see them. Berry huddled tightly with her arms encircling Wow. She looked very small and white with cold. Blood was drying on her face and on the dog's paw. As Calum knelt beside them, Wow struggled to move and whimpered.

"Sh, sh," said Berry. "Good boy. He's got a hurt paw, Calum, he mustn't move." She looked down at the dog, who craned his neck in an effort to lick her. "We're keeping each other warm, aren't we, Wow?"

"They're both a bit knocked about," called Calum to Octavia, "but I think they're more or less okay."

"I'll be back as fast as I can," said Octavia. "Hang in there!" There was a rustle of her waterproof jacket and the squeak of snow as she strode away through the drifts.

"Move over," he said to Berry. He huddled beside her, wishing he'd had more sense than to go off like this with Octavia. He wrapped his jacket as well as he could around both of them, and Berry pulled the dog further into her lap.

"Who was that?" stammered Berry.

"Octavia," he answered, blowing on his fingers.

"Octavia, the Pain?"

"She found you, didn't she? She can't be all bad." He supposed they should get up and do some jumping or something to keep warm, but he couldn't break the tiny squash of warmth that existed in the cramped knot of Berry, the dog, and himself.

"So the dog fell over the edge and you fell after him?" said Calum.

"I heard him before I could see him," she said. "It was horrible, because I could hear him crying and crying and I couldn't find him. Then when I did find him I tried to climb down, but I fell, and my flashlight got smashed up. I tried to find a way out, but there isn't anywhere, I just kept bumping into walls, and Wow was crying, and he couldn't follow me."

Her voice became higher and thinner, and dissolved into tears. Calum put his arm around her a bit awkwardly, still trying to keep the coat around them both.

"We'll soon be home," he said, "there are people out looking for us. Octavia's going to tell them we're here. It won't take long." But even another minute of this would be too long. The wind was rising, and icy blasts were reaching into their sheltering place. Anything was too long to sit in this, so cold and wet he felt ice instead of blood creeping in his veins. He'd never be warm again. They'd probably all get a four star gold award lecture for going out across the moors like this, but he wouldn't mind if it happened in a warm house in dry clothes with a hot drink in his hand. He'd love to be grounded.

"This is where that girl fell down," sniffed Berry. "She never got out."

"Shut up, Berry," said Calum, then felt guilty. "Search parties are better these days than they were then. And Octavia knows where we are."

Berry cuddled the dog more tightly. Calum thought out loud about that long ago night, to focus his mind and distract him from the intensity of cold and damp.

"There was a new son born at Monksmoor House," he said, flexing his fingers and toes to keep them warm. "Myrrh had some mixed-up idea about taking gold, frankincense, and herself to him, so she took the incense box and ran off with it. If they were still doing lights and fireworks, she would have had some idea where the house was."

"Why did she end up in here, then?" murmured Berry wearily.

"Why did you?"

The words seemed to cost her an enormous effort. "I was running after Wow," she said.

Was there a dog in Myrrh's story, too? Sam Bagshaw had been out with his long, dark dog. If he was poaching he would have been on the Monksmoor estate. If Myrrh had managed to get near the house, she might have met them.

"Why did the poacher go out on such a bad night?" wondered Calum.

"No gamekeepers out, I expect," said Berry sleepily. "They were all setting off fireworks and having a drink because of the new baby."

That made sense. It would be a good time for a poacher to check snares, maybe. And if more snow was expected, his tracks would be covered.

"If he'd trapped anything and it stayed in the snare, he wouldn't want to leave it," whispered Berry, "in case something else ate it. Foxes or something." She nestled more comfortably against him like a toddler settling herself for sleep. "And the poacher frightened her. Or the dog."

A very clear picture formed in Calum's mind. Myrrh, clutching the incense box, hurrying across the snow, watching for the lights from Monksmoor House, steadily keeping her course, until she reached the estate.

For the first time, he realized that she wouldn't have taken this route. What had Mark said, the day they went by car to the abbey? *"Monksmoor House is much further to the left, and further back."* In other words, it was nearer to the village than to the main road. From the church, Myrrh would have crossed the moors directly to the house. Perhaps she was even in sight of it. When she turned and ran towards the quarry, its steepest and cruellest drop waited for her.

What did she see as she drew near Monksmoor House? A dim figure that she took for a moorhag? A long, low shape, dark and threatening that growled and barked and ran at her when the moorhag commanded it? So she had turned and fled, not knowing where, running, panting, stumbling, and crying until the ground gave way beneath her feet. . . . He almost wished he had not worked it out.

He cuddled Berry tightly. She, at least, had survived the fall into the quarry.

"This is the shallow end," she murmured, as if she read his thoughts. "It's like a swimming pool. The other end gets much steeper." She yawned and sighed. "When will Octavia find us?"

"Soon," said Calum, but he wished he knew. "We'll shout." Their voices echoed around the stones. It made him think of Mark and Drew, and the abbey, and Mark's speech.

"Give me your hands, Berry," he said. "All right, one hand at a time if you have to hang on to the dog." Chafing the heat into Berry's frozen hands at least took his mind off his own stinging toes and fingers. Berry was yawning again.

"Don't go to sleep," he said, so frozen that he could hardly tell which were his own fingers and which were hers. "We need to stay awake for the rescue party." But her yawns were infectious. The cold and long walk had drained him. It seemed impossible that anyone could be so cold and wet and uncomfortable and still fall asleep, but his eyes wanted to close.

"We've got to stay awake, Myrrh," he said, but she was falling asleep against his shoulder and it seemed heartless to wake her. "Shout for help once more."

He shouted, but she only half woke up and murmured, "You called me Myrrh."

He shuffled to ease the stiffness in his freezing legs. Through numb and clumsy lips he began to mutter his multiplication tables to keep himself awake. Then he thought the Lord's Prayer might be more use, so he said that, but found he was drifting into sleep before the end.

"God, if you're up there, please get us out of this," he whispered. He chafed at a cold hand between his own hands. Myrrh's hand was freezing. But she wasn't Myrrh; she was Berry. . . . Was he falling asleep again? He forced his eyes open.

He tried to repeat Mark's speech in the Octave, but "Let Beckerton be a place of warmth and welcome" seemed to laugh at him now. Then he was curling up at Aunt Dorcas's fireside . . . then he realized he had been dreaming . . . he curled his hands and dug his fingernails into his palms. Pain might keep him awake.

Play the postcard game. Beckerton, he thought. *Home of Dogs*

108

and Darkness. Danger and D — no. Don't think of that.

Somebody was watching them. He could feel it. Almost too cold, stiff, and exhausted to move, Calum raised his head. A beam of light showed a figure standing opposite them, at the edge of the quarry. Somebody who held a light, and had seen them, because the light fell in Calum's eyes and made him blink. A tall figure, in a long, rough tunic.

"Mark!" yelled Calum, and suddenly found he had the strength to shout loudly, and keep shouting. "Mark, we're here! Berry, it's all right! It's Mark!" And from somewhere, dimly and far off, came the voices of Octavia, Nick, and Melanie, all calling their names, and Wow slowly raised his head and beat his tail on the ground.

Eleven

Being rescued didn't mean being warm straightaway. There was still a long, confused struggle of shouting voices, ropes being thrown down, and Nick inching down the cliff to help winch Berry and Wow to safety. Octavia's face was white in the light of the flashlights. Somebody—probably Tom—blew a whistle to let other rescuers know that they were found. By the time Nick came back for him, Calum found he was so cramped he couldn't move without help, and the pain of straightening his freezing limbs gripped him and forced him to wince. But finally, at the top, the strong arms pulling him up and wrapping him in a hug were his father's.

"Sorry," stammered Calum, and his eyes blurred. He was glad it was dark.

"It's all right," said his father, still holding him. "You're all right."

Peggy was with them, and some of the students. As the other rescue parties joined them he found his mother was there, tearful and hugging him as if she never dared let him go. And everyone was hugging him, and hugging Berry, putting blankets around them and giving them something warm to drink. Then at last they were put on sleds and pulled, or, where necessary, carried across the snow, and they were back to a part of the moors he thought he recognized, then there was the main road, the farm track, the village, the lane, the house, and the fireside he had thought he would never see again. Aunt Dorcas looked so much older, and so worried, as he staggered through the door, that he felt sorry for her.

"Into the bath with you!" she commanded.

Lying back in the steamy water he began at last to feel truly warm again. Heat soaked deep into his bones. The tips of his toes were red, and there were scratches on his hands. His mother had insisted that somebody stayed with him in case he fell asleep or fainted in the bath, so his father sat on the floor and listened to his account of all that had happened. He didn't interrupt, and Calum wondered when the thunderbolt was going to fall—but it didn't.

His eyes wanted to close. He hauled himself out of the bath, dried himself, and dragged his way up to his attic where his mother was waiting.

"How's Berry?" he asked as he crawled into bed.

"Peggy's done some first aid," said his mother. "We hope the doctor might get through tomorrow."

"Where's Mark?" he asked. It seemed strange, come to think of it, that he hadn't seen Mark among the flock of rescuers.

"Mark? I've no idea," said his mother. "Home, I should

hope."

An hour ago he had been stranded, frozen to the icy cliff. And that cold, cruel quarry was still out there, yawning up at the falling snow. There was only a windowpane between Calum and the vast cold air, but now he was in his own world, a place of clean sheets, gentle light, and all his own familiar things.

He didn't want to fall asleep. He wanted to lie here, more than ever aware of comfort and warmth. The pillow was a cloud under his head. He was swathed in clouds.

"Leave the curtains open," he said. From the safety of his bed he wanted to see the sky. Was Myrrh sleeping in the chill of the churchyard, or was she dancing in the stars on a winter night, free forever?

⌖ ⌖ ⌖

When he woke in the morning he couldn't believe the clock. He thought at first that there must be something wrong with it. But his watch said the same, and the church clock chimed the half hour. He threw off the covers and scrabbled in the drawer for clean clothes. Dressed and running downstairs, he heard voices in the kitchen. One was his father's, but the other was Major Shipley's.

"Great," muttered Calum. "Two thousand lashes before breakfast." He may as well get it over. He paused to straighten his hair and sweater before opening the door.

"Good morning, Major Shipley," he said. "I'm . . . oh! Hi, Octavia."

What was she doing here? Was she only there to watch her grandfather chase him out of the village, or something? When his mother and Aunt Dorcas came in from the garden and banged the door he jumped, and decided he'd better speak first.

"I'm sorry, Major Shipley," he said.

"Sorry?" said Major Shipley, with a dark frown on his face. "You're sorry? Octavia told me what happened. She's the one who went running off across the moors in the middle of the night, and you wouldn't let her go alone. And it was you who finished up shivering at the bottom of a cliff with little Berry. What have you got to be sorry about? I'm most grateful to you!" He shook Calum's hand with a powerful grip, and clapped him on the shoulder. Calum cast a bewildered look at Octavia.

"Sorry, Calum," she said primly from behind her grandfather's back. Then she crossed her eyes and mouthed "poacher," but she was grinning like a fellow conspirator.

"It wasn't all Octavia's fault," said Calum. "I gave in and went after her. If I hadn't done that, she might have changed her mind and come back."

"I very much doubt it," said Major Shipley. The kettle, which had been steaming gently, switched itself off, and Calum's mom swished hot water around the teapot. Aunt Dorcas asked what everyone would like to drink and whether Calum wanted breakfast, lunch, or both.

"How's Berry?" he asked, and forgot to put milk on his cereal.

"I hear she's cut and bruised with a very swollen wrist,"

said Aunt Dorcas, "but she'll do. Drew looked after Wow. He's making the most of having a hurt leg, but he'll mend. Oh, and we had such a terrific party last night, until half the village and most of the American Embassy went off to the moors. The Americans went away after church this morning. They had a splendid time."

"I do hope they'll come back," said Major Shipley. "They should become a regular part of the Octave."

Calum looked up in astonishment with his mouth full of muesli. If he hadn't heard Major Shipley say that himself, he would never have believed it.

"I might go and see Berry later," said Calum.

"I'll come with you if you do," said Octavia, and enjoyed seeing him splutter.

"And I'll go to Myrrh's grave," said Aunt Dorcas. "There's winter jasmine in flower at the front door, so she can have some of that."

"So it's . . . ," Calum stopped, and swallowed hard, "so it's you? The one who leaves flowers on Myrrh's grave?"

Aunt Dorcas smiled sadly into her coffee. "My mother used to do it," she said, "so now I do. Myrrh was her friend."

"I've worked it out, Aunt Dorcas," said Calum. "Myrrh was taking the gold box of frankincense and herself to the new baby at Monksmoor House — she got the Christmas story mixed up with her own. But Sam Bagshaw was out with his dog and ordered it to chase her away." It seemed that the only way to clear Myrrh's name was to accuse his own family. "He must have wanted her to think she'd seen a moorhag with a demon dog, so that she'd run for it and not recognize him. She would have believed in all that, so it worked, but she panicked and kept running until she fell into the quarry. When she was found dead Sam must have worked out how she got there, but he couldn't tell anyone without giving himself away. All his life, he let them think Myrrh was just a thief." He wished Sam Bagshaw hadn't been his great-great-grandfather. "Sorry, Aunt Dorcas."

"Well, it's hardly your fault if my grandfather was a rascal," she said. "And we always knew that's what he was. Why don't you finish your breakfast and go and help your father shovel snow? Or get the sled, or something. Major Shipley, don't you think — it's a hundred years and more since Myrrh died — don't you think she should be painted into the frescoes, where she belonged? The third king's servant should have been Myrrh."

"I don't know if there's a photograph of her," he said. "Somebody might have one. We can ask around. It's time she was remembered with kindness. You'd think our ancestors valued a box more than a child. I don't know what they were thinking of."

"And if we don't find a picture," said Aunt Dorcas, "Berry can model for her."

"It's time we went," said Major Shipley. "By the way, Calum, I hear you play badminton. I'll book a court at Westcastle Leisure Center for next weekend. If Octavia won't play you, I will. And bring Mark."

✤   ✤   ✤

Late in the afternoon, Calum went with Aunt Dorcas and stood back while she arranged flowers on Myrrh's grave. The snow was forming ice crystals that dazzled into the late light. Calum, turning, saw a familiar tall figure striding up to the church.

"Mark!" He clambered through the snow to meet Mark at the church gate. "So you got to the abbey last night!"

"It was brilliant," said Mark, and his eyes were shining. "What's all this I've heard about you?"

"Tell me about the abbey," said Calum.

"I thought I'd die of cold on the way there," said Mark, "but I wasn't going to say so to Dad and Mr. Shipley. We stopped at Monksmoor House, and they've got this wonderful four-wheel drive thing. The road from there to the abbey wasn't too bad, and they got us there. Some of the staff came to watch, and the people who live near the abbey, so we had some sort of a crowd to watch. The speech sounded . . . ," he gave a gesture that was half a shrug and half a shiver, and slowed down. "It sounded wonderful, but it was as if I didn't control it. It was nothing to do with me. Something was happening to me—it was like having another voice. Or another me. Strange. Good, but strange."

He glanced at his boots, as if he wasn't sure how to cope with all this, then went on, "We went back to Monksmoor House, and they asked if we'd like to stay the night. Better than walking back across the moor. So we did. Four-star hotel, hot shower, television in bed!"

"But," said Calum, trying to work it out, "was that before

or after you were at the quarry?"

Mark looked at him as if he were speaking Greek. "I wasn't anywhere near the quarry."

"Yes, you were, just before the rest of the rescue party came. I was there with Berry and Wow. I looked up, and you were there—just you, by yourself—you had a flashlight or something. You were wearing your costume."

For a few solemn seconds, Mark said nothing. Then he spoke slowly.

"Calum, believe me, I was never at the quarry last night. I was always with Dad and Mr. Shipley, never on my own. And no way would I go trekking across the moors in a dress! I got changed, remember? I took it with me, put it on when we got to the abbey, and took it off again as soon as we'd finished."

"But I know what I saw!" said Calum. His hands were tingling.

Mark laid a hand on Calum's shoulder. "I'm not doubting what you saw, Calum. But it wasn't me."

Neither of them said anything.

Aunt Dorcas picked her way carefully through the icy patches towards them. Mark and Calum went to meet her and help her stay on her feet.

"Everyone has been saying what a good Octave it was this year, in spite of everything," said Aunt Dorcas. "The Americans were a tremendous hit. And I hear great things about your speech at the abbey, Mark. A pity there weren't more there to hear it. Maybe there will be, next year."

Mark nodded at Calum. "He'll do it next year," he said.

117

"Yes, you will, Calum. It's come to you, now. You wait and see. Nobody will try to stop you. It'll be different, after this."

"It's already different," said Aunt Dorcas firmly, and smiled deeply among the peachstone wrinkles. "We really kept The Octave of Angels. Mark braved ice and snow to say what had to be said, because it mattered. And most of the village got off its bottom to help Berry and let the students help, too. Perhaps we're finally working out what the Octave is for."

"It only took seven hundred years," muttered Calum.

Aunt Dorcas chuckled. "Don't expect miracles," she said. "We're still the same people. We haven't turned into Sweet-Murmurings-Round-the-Beck overnight. We're still an odd assortment of people who wouldn't choose to live together — we just happen to live in the same village. But we've taken a big step in the right direction."

"It's more than that," said Mark quietly. He seemed to have grown up overnight. "Something happened, last night. Something changed. Something broke."

"Yes," said Aunt Dorcas, "and you were both part of what happened, whatever it was."

Beckerton, thought Calum. *Home of . . .* what? Anything seemed possible, now.

At the gate, Aunt Dorcas paused to adjust her grip on Mark's arm. She looked up at the setting sun as if she shared a secret with it.

"It'll be dark soon," she said. "What a beautiful, fiery sunset! Look at that sky!"

118

Calum looked. The last of the afternoon sunlight flared golden over the village and caught the sparkle of snow on treetops, on walls, and far off on the wintry moors. It was as if the snow had caught fire.